Holt's eyes were drawn to the horrifying creature in the center of the great room. The beast crouched like a monstrous wolf, tail lashing, jaws slavering as it crept toward the weeping barmaid.

This wasn't a normal animal. There was something grotesque in the muscles rippling along its back and forelegs, an unnatural menace in the gurgling sounds it made. Reaching forward with almost human dexterity, the creature extended long, hooked claws from each fur-cloaked forepaw.

"Stop it! Leave her alone!" Holt shouted. He grasped at his belt, only then remember~~~~ left his blade back in the ~~~~

Quest Triad
Douglas Niles

Pawns Prevail
Book I

Suitors Duel
Book II

Immortal Game
Book III

Other FIRST QUEST™
Young Readers Adventures

Rogues to Riches
J. Robert King

The Unicorn Hunt
Elaine Cunningham

Son of Dawn
Dixie McKeone

Summerhill Hounds
J. Robert King

First Quest™

Books

Immortal Game

Book III of the Quest Triad

Douglas Niles

IMMORTAL GAME

Copyright © 1996 TSR, Inc.
All Rights Reserved.

Cover art by Don Clavette.

First Printing: February 1996
Printed in the United States of America
Library of Congress Catalog Card Number: 95-62072

9 8 7 6 5 4 3 2 1

ISBN: 0-7869-0478-X
8157XXX1501

TSR, Inc.
201 Sheridan Springs Rd.
Lake Geneva, WI 53147
United States of America

TSR Ltd.
120 Church End, Cherry Hinton
Cambridge CB1 3LB
United Kingdom

To those who keep their faith until the end,
and especially Megan, Sara, and Katie.

Prologue

"We would like to hear an explanation from your own lips," said the gold dragon, his deep voice rumbling through the Immortal Hall. The huge, shimmering serpent was coiled easily on the seat of honor in the center of a marbled amphitheater. Whiskers drooped regally to either side of his broad head, forming a golden mane that now framed a fierce scowl. Mighty claws drumming restlessly on the slick, marble floor, the wyrm cleared his throat in a menacing growl. "Is it true you have played the Mortal Game?"

"Only once!" Dalliphree blurted. "The other

time we just watched!" Her wings buzzed noisily as she bobbed her head in affirmation, bravely meeting her inquisitor's frowning gaze.

Beside Dalli, Pusanth sighed in resignation. The white-bearded old sage slumped his shoulders, but the fairy wasn't ready to quit yet.

She looked up from the plain wooden bench, well below the raised seats of the immortal judges. The empty rows of the amphitheater rose in alabaster rings beyond.

I feel like a minnow in a fishbowl, she thought.

Dalliphree had difficulty staying on the bench— her wings wanted to buzz her right up into the air. Yet she sensed that if she allowed that to happen, she—and Pusanth too—would be in even more trouble than they already were.

The sage reached over then and firmly grabbed her flowered belt, as if he wanted to make sure she stayed right there.

"You probably think it's *all* my fault!" Dalli sulked. That was so unfair—the trouble they were in was only *mostly* her fault.

"Only once?" came the dragon's dubious response.

Before answering that stern voice, Dalli looked for mercy among the other judges. To one side of the dragon stood a centaur, huffily stomping his front hooves. The creature's human face—wrinkled by age, draped with a white beard—glowered even more sternly than the dragon's. The centaur's arms were crossed on his chest, while his horse tail swished back and forth in agitation.

On the dragon's other flank sat a thin, elderly elf, long hair fading to white, yet still glowing with strands of sunlit yellow. His green eyes squinted through tiny spectacles, twinkling with a hint of humor that softened his disapproving frown.

The final member of the council, a tall knight clad in full plate armor stood in aloof silence some distance from the elf. The featureless metal visor was closed over his face, a fact that made him the most intimidating member of the panel.

Dalli shivered, turning her eyes from the frightening and warlike visage.

No mercy here.

A cool breeze wafted between the marble columns that ringed the entire, roofless theater, and the scent of lilac filled the vast bowl. Beyond the stonework arches, puffy clouds drifted through blue skies, and the tinkle of gentle music was carried on the wind.

How nice it would be to just fly away, Dalli thought—over the fields and hills of the immortal realms. . . .

When Dalli failed to respond, Pusanth spoke up. "We played the game . . . once." Pusanth repeated Dalli's assertion, looking at her so sternly that she was forced to pay attention.

The dragon's eyebrows rose, and the centaur snorted impatiently. The knight stood silent and impassive, and the elf tightened his lips against an involuntary smile. "Tell us about the *one* time, then," he said, not unkindly.

"Well, it was Pusanth's idea—" chirped the fairy.

"What? I beg to differ!" The old sage's voice quavered with outrage.

"Well—you didn't argue about it! I said 'let's play', and you said 'all right'!"

"Ahem." The dragon merely cleared his throat, but it was enough to silence the bickering pair. "Never mind about whose idea it was—tell us what happened."

"Well, it was pretty harmless," Dalli continued, with barely a pause for breath. "We picked our mortals—I chose a beautiful princess, Pusanth this boring farmboy who makes cheese. Like usual in the Mortal Game, we just made a wager and watched them in their simple little lives, playing our tokens now and then. Nothing we did made much difference—I played a bee sting on the boy's horse, and a little gust of wind. Pusanth got the greenleaf play, and he made some fungus grow so the boy could see underground. Can we go now?"

"Were those the *only* plays?" demanded the centaur, snorting.

"Oh—did I forget to mention the artifact?" Dalliphree asked sweetly.

"And the seven directions of chaos," Pusanth said with a sigh. "I suspect that those are the

4

plays that have drawn your attention. I knew that we shouldn't have—!"

"The time for regrets is well past," said the dragon with a touch of rebuke. "You are right—it is the artifact that has drawn our attention. But what is this about chaos?"

"Oh, that's over," the fairy said breezily. "I made the artifact to give to the princess, and Pusanth used his chaos play to make it go wild. But it ended happily—the princess got the artifact, and I won the game."

"And she is still in possession of this artifact?" the knight inquired, speaking in a deep, rasping voice that emerged with surprising force from behind the steel visor.

"Naturally. I mean, of course she is. Why, the Crown of Vanderthan is so powerful that if she lost it, we'd certainly hear about it. The forces of Entropy could use it to take over all Karawenn—or any other world. *Sure*, she's still got it." Only then did it occur to Dalliphree that her argument had not exactly strengthened her defense. "That is, unless she broke it or something," she added lamely.

"I've said this before, Yizillay," the centaur said, addressing the gold dragon. "That artifact token is too powerful. If we *have* to allow the Mortal Game—and I, for one, think that we don't—at the very least let's remove that option. In the hands of an irresponsible immortal, the results can be disastrous!"

"Hey! We haven't had any disaster yet!" the fairy objected.

"I fear it is only a matter of time," Yizillay declared seriously. "We have learned that the creatures of Entropy—all the dark and unnatural denizens of Karawenn—have been called to a quest that puts that entire world at risk. Their assigned task is to capture the Crown of Vander-than."

"Oh. Well—the princess can take good care of—"

"That's not the point," the dragon interrupted with, for him, unseemly haste.

"No," Pusanth agreed with a sigh. He looked at the fairy seated beside him. "It's that—because of our game—we've condemned Karawenn to another bloody war. And that's not right."

Dalliphree pouted silently. She started to argue, then sighed. "I guess you're right," she admitted.

"So." The dragon spoke with an air of finality, glad that the discussion was at last proceeding. "The only thing to do is to have the mortals destroy the crown. Then the problem will be finished. Do you agree?"

"Yes!" declared Pusanth.

"Well, it sounds a little drastic to me," said the fairy. "After all, she's got it locked up in the castle. How can the forces of Entropy get it there?"

"You know that Entropy can travel in any disguise—evil can be encountered in a human or elf just as easily as in a drooling monster. As long as the crown exists, it cannot be considered safe," the elven elder said benignly. "I'm afraid the others are right. The mortals must be warned—and the crown must be destroyed."

"Warned? Like in a dream?" asked the fairy enthusiastically.

"No!" barked Yizillay. "We know how you sprites are with dreams. It should be something simpler—animal messengers!"

"Animals? *Talking* animals?" Dalli suggested with a coy smile.

"Two words, only," said the elf. "And the message can be sent to each mortal for three heartbeats of time, no more."

"That will be fine," Pusanth said, overruling Dalli's objection. "We can reach the Daryman and the dwarf—"

"And the First Daughter, and that elf, and the king of Vanderthan—there's *lots* of people to tell!" Dalliphree chimed in.

"You are the maker of the artifact," the knight said to Dalli, his powerful voice silencing her cheery outburst. "Now you must tell us how it can be destroyed."

"Like, *really* destroyed?" Dalliphree stalled.

"Yes—*really* destroyed!" The centaur, eyes narrowed, pierced the fairy with his stare. "I hope you are not about to tell us that it is indestructible!

You know what an infraction of the rules *that* would be!"

"Of course it's not indestructible!" the fairy retorted. "Why, the very idea that I would do something so reckless—"

"Tell us, then." The knight's tone was unnecessarily dire and menacing, Dalliphree thought. His question stabbed her like a sword: "How can it be destroyed?"

"Well, there is *one* way." But it was such a pretty crown, and a wondrous creation. The fairy was reluctant to answer, so she tried one of her favorite tactics: stalling. "It will be kind of difficult, though. Dangerous, too. In fact, it's kind of a secret. . . ."

* * * * *

The dark passage twisted between stained, rocky walls. A lone figure, clad in metal armor, stalked along the dank corridor. Though the visor remained closed across his face, the knight had no difficulty steering his way through inky blackness. He entered a small alcove, where he unlocked a metal-strapped box and carefully drew out the cloth-wrapped sphere within.

Setting the object on a shelf of rock, the knight lifted the visor of his helm to reveal a face as pallid and lifeless as any corpse's—except for his lips, which were full, their color the bright crimson of fresh blood. Around him, all was darkness, for he huddled in a corner of the immortal realm where light could never reach.

Removing his gauntlets, reaching with skeletal hands, the hideous warrior pulled back the cloth to reveal a crystal ball, dimly glowing upon its black surface of rock. Those fingers, thin as bone, could have crushed the treasured globe with ease, yet they held it now with gentle care, stroking the surface as a red glow slowly fired within.

"Xtan . . . my mighty ally," hissed the knight, his breath thick with the musty stench of carrion. "I have news of the Crown of Vanderthan."

Slowly, the fiery image in the globe clarified into a proud, reptilian head—a visage covered in crimson scales, leering with potent evil. The dragon's eyes burned within that blood-red face. "Speak, Karnach."

"The mortals of Karawenn are warned of your intentions. They have sensed your agents abroad, know that the crown is endangered."

"And?"

"We believe the mortals will make every effort to destroy the artifact." The knight's voice carried as a harsh whisper.

"Have you learned how this can be done?" rasped the dragon.

"No—the accursed fairy, for once, kept her mouth shut. But I shall discover the truth."

"Do that—quickly!" The fury in the dragon's

tone seemed to heat the globe beneath the knight's clawlike hands. "And in the meantime, here on Karawenn, I shall set the forces of Entropy to the task. . . ."

1
Graywall

The blades met with a ringing clash. The young swordsman stepped backward, giving ground against the dwarf's steady slashes. Still, the lean and beardless warrior fought patiently, avoiding the mistakes of immaturity. He bore his sword—which had an unusual blade of dull, stony gray—deftly, striking often but never leaving himself vulnerable to a sudden counterattack.

The dwarven warrior was broad shouldered and well muscled, and held a short sword in each hand. His beard bristled around a red, glowing scar on his cheek, and his eyes glared fiercely as he

11

pressed an abrupt attack. The sturdy, stout-legged warrior stabbed first with one blade, then slashed quickly with the other.

A cloudless sky, pale with early morning sun, soared above the combatants, and a horizon of rugged mountains fully encircled them. The pair fought on a wide stone plaza—one of many such balconies staggered along the lip and walls of a plunging canyon. A battlement lined the cliff wall above them, and several heavy iron doors were framed firmly in the bedrock of the sheer mountainside.

Abruptly the human ceased his retreat, bringing that gray blade around in an apparently desperate sweep. The dwarf raised one sword to parry and drew back the other for a deadly thrust—but at the last minute the human reversed his attack, coming high over the dwarf's parry, driving toward his armored chest. With a nimble flick of his wrist the man brought his blade against his opponent's and twisted.

One short sword went flying, and the other flailed widely out of the way. The dwarf looked down, saw the stony blade poised an inch from his heart. With a grunt, he lowered the second blade, bowed to the man, and then turned to another dwarf who leaned casually against the wall, watching the duel.

"He's got the best of me the last five times," groused the dwarven swordsman. "I tell you, Fen-

rald—there's nothing more I can teach him!"
Despite his growling tone, the dwarf's voice held a
hint of surprise—and respect.

"Well done, lad," chuckled the dwarven observer,
a gleam of pride brightening his eye. "I told you,
Dasswalt, he's a quick study."

The burly dwarf nodded. "Considering he's been
in Graywall for only half a year, it's amazing he's
learned any more than the basics. I've had dwarven apprentices work with me for more than a
decade and—I hate to admit this—this young man
has learned more over one winter than those
dwarves could in ten!"

Holton Jaken, still tingling from the excitement
of the mock duel, flushed at the compliment, then
bowed. "Thank you, Master Dasswalt." Looking at
the stout, gray-bladed sword in his hand, Holt felt
the familiar touch of awe. "Fate has given me the
Lodestone Blade . . . I'd like to think I might bear it
with some small measure of skill."

He thought of the others who had wielded the
potent weapon, Darymen of Oxvale through four
centuries. Commoners all, they had been men of
freedom, each honored to bear the sword of the
magical gray, stone blade. These folk had long
since renounced the authority of their king, as well
as any lesser nobles. Under a heritage of equality
and pride, a succession of Darymen had borne the
Lodestone Blade for all those years. Often they
had fought in service of the monarch, but never—

and this was an important distinction—at his command.

Weaponmaster Dasswalt departed the balcony, pushing open the heavy iron doors leading to his arsenal within the mountain. Fenrald and Holt, meanwhile, wandered across the wide stone platform in the shadows of the craggy peaks rising to the west. Beyond the balcony wall, a cliff plunged into a canyon so deep its bottom was lost in mist. A series of similar vantages and portals lined the cliff face—below, above, and beside this one—each providing light to the delved dwarven city of Graywall.

High, arching bridges of stone spanned the great chasm in two places. A few paths twisted along the cliffs, leading to the balconies, but every approach to the city was guarded by numerous strongpoints—squat battle towers and small, walled enclosures that gave defenders a vantage above the exposed and precipitous trails.

Though a wonder of caverns, caves, and vast chambers lay within the metal doors, the Daryman preferred these plazas, with their sweeping vistas of the Trollheight Mountains and the deep canyon.

The dwarf looked with a pensive expression at the young man, his friend. Holt's eyes remained focused on the distant sky, beyond even the peaks where snowfields blazed in pastoral reflection and slick, jagged summits of rock sparkled like facets of obsidian.

"It's so . . . peaceful, quiet," mused the young man. "Even more serene than the millpond back in Oxvale."

"Are you getting homesick?" Fenrald asked after a pause. Holt suspected the dwarf already knew the answer.

"I miss my father, the other Darymen—even Nowell the Aching," the young man said with a laugh, remembering friends and good food . . . fishing in the stream, hunting in the Knollbarrens. Then his eyes grew serious as he remembered the one he missed most of all.

"It's been seven months, and I still recall everything about the way she looks—and sounds, and smells. I thought that time might help, might make me see that I'm a fool."

"There's nothing foolish about love, lad."

"Yes there is!" snapped the Daryman with real bitterness. "There is when I'm in love with a woman who can never love me back!" Even as he spoke, he knew the words were unfair.

"It's her curse to be born a princess," Fenrald offered gently.

"Or mine—born to the farm! But either way, there's no future for us. The king made that plenty clear."

"Try to think of something else," the dwarf said awkwardly, clearing his throat as if he sensed the uselessness of his own suggestion.

Holt turned to him and spoke with real anguish.

"I've tried, my friend—tried every day, every night of this winter and spring." He sighed, and it was as if all the air had flowed out of his lungs, shriveling him to a frail skeleton.

"By the Spheres, how I've tried! And the only thing I've learned is that it doesn't do any good."

His fingers clenched into fists as Holt spun back toward the edge of the balcony, staring into the vast gulf of Graywall Canyon. A deep chill lingered there in the snow-covered swath of river so far below. That coldness seemed to extend into the Daryman's body, and his heart.

Movement flashed in the sky, and the plunging shape of a hawk caught his eye—a harrier swooping past a pigeon. The smaller bird squawked and twirled away, while the soaring predator continued downward, wings tucked.

The Daryman felt a growing sense of anticipation as he stood beside the battlement, watching the hawk. The hooked beak gaped as a shrill cry pierced the air—and at first Holt couldn't believe his ears. He whirled to see Fenrald staring in astonishment after the bird. Only then did the bird's cry echo from the far wall of the canyon, and Holt knew that he wasn't losing his mind.

"*Danis.*" The first cry was the name of the First Daughter, clearly articulated. Knowing what he would hear, Holt nevertheless strained to catch the next echo.

"*Crown.*"

The harrier was gone, plummeting into the canyon, no doubt gliding easily through the shadowy depths. Yet even as the echo of the two words faded into the still morning air, Holt was seized by a fear so powerful, so overwhelming, that it left him only one clear choice of action.

"I've got to go to Vanderton," the Daryman declared. "There's danger—"

"I know," replied the grim-faced dwarf. "I heard it too."

"And *felt* it! Fear, for Danis."

Fenrald nodded. "I'll come with you. We can be on the trail in an hour."

Holt nodded in gratitude, deeply moved by his friend's offer—but the dwarf simply harrumphed something about getting packed.

It took them less than an hour to gather their belongings: ropes, waterskins, and dried foods, all wrapped in a bundle of bedrolls, spare cloaks, and a tarp. Holt saddled Old Thunder, the big farm horse that had served him so well, and strapped the roll of equipment across the steed's haunches.

Meanwhile Fenrald prepared his small pony for riding, talking gruffly to the placid mare. The shaggy little mount had been a gift from Princess Danis, and though the dwarf had never named it, Holt knew his companion had become quite fond of the animal during their autumn trek from Vanderton to Graywall.

Now they set out to reverse that journey, with

real urgency. Holt left the dwarven city behind with a sense of wistful remembrance, wondering if he would ever see the place again. Graywall's hospitality had touched him, but now the compulsion of the hawk-borne warning forced all regrets aside. With waves to Dasswalt and many other friends the Daryman had made over the winter, the two riders started along the mountain trail.

For three days, they rapidly descended through mountain valleys. Every hour brought them farther down from the icebound heights, as if weeks of spring advanced during the course of a day. By the time they traversed the last foothills and approached the River Tannyv, Karawenn was in full bloom around them. Verdant leaves weighed down the hardwoods of Greenbriar Forest, and flowers danced in the riverbank marshes, swaying to every tickle of breeze. The fragrance of a thousand blossoms sweetened the air, a windborne perfume.

Still, foreboding shrouded them both. Their fear for the princess, the apprehension that some terrible threat lurked before them, drove them hard along the trail.

"Nothing's happened yet—not to her, or the kingdom," Fenrald assured Holt a dozen times. "We'd have heard any bad news even in Graywall."

"I know," said the Daryman, inwardly trembling—*not yet, but when?*

On the fourth night of their trek, they

approached a riverside inn. The sign over the door announced the place to be the Catfish Inn, and since both of the travelers were ready for cooked meals and indoor beds, Holt and Fenrald wearily turned their horses over to a stableboy and trudged into the large, airy common room.

Holt paid the innkeeper a silver coin, which covered their lodging and two meals, as well as the keeping of their horses. Fenrald, meanwhile, bought a foaming pitcher of ale and carried it to a table in the corner. One mud-stained traveler sat nearby, but otherwise this part of the room was empty.

Sitting down with a groan of pleasure, Holt stretched his feet out and allowed his stiff chair to massage some of the kinks out of his back. He sipped a small glass of the beer, while Fenrald drank right out of the pitcher. For a few minutes, they rested in silence, slowly warming to the feel of civilized surroundings. A barmaid brought them platters of bread, potatoes, and meat, and they devoured the food like famished wild animals.

They didn't notice a cloaked figure rise from his small table beside the door, though Holt looked up curiously as the stranger approached their table. He wore a long cape of green and a cowled hood that all but covered his head. Only a strip of his forehead—and a pair of flashing blue eyes—showed as the stranger bowed politely.

"Might a weary traveler join you two lords?" the fellow inquired, his tone slightly mocking—but not unfriendly. At the same time, his eyes made a remarkable shift in color—from the blue of a placid sea to the viridescent green of a flawless emerald.

"Not lords, but you're wel—" Abruptly, and with a flash of delight, Holt recognized those eyes. "Syssal!" he cried, leaping up to sweep the elf into an embrace. The muddy traveler who sat nearby apparently took no note of their conversation—he just hunched lower over his ale, adjusting his leather mantle over broad shoulders.

"Your disguise almost fooled me!" admitted the Daryman.

The elf smiled, displaying the magical golden band about one of his fingers. "My ring, as always, aids me," Syssal said, pulling back his hood enough that they could see the handsome, narrow face. Holt knew that the magical circlet allowed the elf to assume virtually any appearance he desired.

Syssal frowned in concern. "It seems that, once again, we travel the Tannyv Valley."

"Aye," Fenrald grunted quietly. "Under less than happy circumstances, on our part."

"It was a fox who spoke to me—barking *words*, I swear it!—warning of danger to the princess and the crown," whispered the elf.

"We heard a hawk." Tension thrummed in Holt's voice. "Crying the same thing—danger to Danis, and the artifact. If only she had never found that crown!"

Syssal quietly raised a finger to his lips as Fenrald noisily drained his pitcher. "I'm for bed," the dwarf declared gruffly.

"Me, too. Do you have a room?" Holt asked Syssal. When the elf shook his head, the Daryman invited him to share their quarters, and the three climbed the narrow staircase to the small, wood-paneled room.

"Too many ears down there," the dwarf suggested when they had the door securely closed behind them. Holt kicked off his boots and hung his sword from a hook beside the door, nodding as Fenrald continued. "Something tells me we ought to keep our concerns quiet, for the time being."

"That makes good sense—"

The elf's reply was interrupted by a scream of terror from downstairs. The trio heard something heavy crash to the floor, then more cries. The sounds were shrill with panic, but rising above the din came savage noises—growling, bestial roars, expelled by some monstrously inhuman throat.

Holt threw open the door, racing for the head of the stairs. He looked down into the great room and saw a wreckage of tables and chairs. The maid who had served them cowered behind the bar.

The Daryman's eyes were drawn to the horrifying creature in the center of the great room. The beast crouched like a monstrous wolf, tail lashing, jaws slavering as it crept toward the weeping barmaid.

This wasn't a normal animal, nor even a warwolf. There was something grotesque in the muscles rippling along its back and forelegs, an unnatural menace in the gurgling sounds. Reaching forward with almost human dexterity, the creature extended long, hooked claws from each fur-cloaked forepaw.

"Stop it! Leave her alone!" Holt shouted. He grasped at his belt, only then remembering he had left his blade back in the room.

The monster whirled to face him, and in one quick pounce started up the stairs. The Daryman stumbled backward as another leap carried the beast all the way to the second floor landing. Red eyes glowing, the wolfish creature snarled wetly, drooling a long tongue between sharp white fangs.

"Back up! Don't let it bite you!" Syssal Kipican shouted urgently, and the Daryman sensed there was more at risk here than wounding or loss of blood. The beast was so hideously unnatural, so fierce and purposeful, that it could only be a creature of Entropy.

He saw tattered traces of a mud-spattered leather mantle on the brute's burly shoulders, and he remembered the man who had worn that cloak in the great room—he had been sitting very near the three companions.

The wolf-creature crept forward, eyes glittering with cruel pleasure as Holt backed along the hallway.

"Here!" Fenrald's voice pulled the Daryman around, and he nimbly caught the Lodestone Blade when the dwarf tossed it to him.

The monster leapt, and the gray blade caught it full in the face. Holt stumbled backward, barely avoiding the rip of those awful claws as the wounded brute tumbled to the floor with a strangled yelp.

Again it crouched, growling and drooling, and this time Holt knew what he had to do. The Daryman stepped forward, raising the weapon, feinting right—and then chopping viciously from the left as the monster roared and attacked. The cut was true, and deep. With a pathetic snarl, the creature collapsed to the floor, dead.

Hesitantly, the Daryman knelt, stunned by the monster's horrific appearance, sickened and yet strangely fascinated by its grotesque features. As he reached a hand toward the savage, brutal face, that visage changed before his eyes.

In another moment he found himself looking down at the body of a man. Even with only a dim memory of the stranger downstairs, he knew this was the muddy traveler who had sat at the nearby table.

"A werewolf." Syssal Kipican made the statement, approaching Holt and the corpse in the silent wreckage of the inn.

"What?" The Daryman had never heard the term.

"A . . . disease, or perhaps a curse. The moon is full tonight, isn't it?"

"Aye," remembered Fenrald.

"This being had once been a man. Corrupted by evil, it was cursed to become a beast. The disease can transform a person into a wolf—and, I've heard, sometimes a giant rat, as well. It is the full moon that brings these creatures into full frenzy."

"A man changes from human to wolf against his will?" Holt asked with a shudder of revulsion. He looked at the corpse with a measure of sympathy.

"Yes. And the mere fact of this one's presence is very bad news."

"Why do you say that?" asked Holt, suppressing an uncanny chill.

"Werewolves, like the undead, are potent servants of the dark force. This can only mean that Entropy is already abroad in Karawenn."

2
Return to Vanderton

Syssal rode behind Holt. The elf's slight weight
was no added burden for Old Thunder, and the
three travelers were back on the trail with the
dawn. A few villages dotted the long road down the
Tannyv Valley, but the riders found these clusters
of farms and cottages unnaturally quiet; windows
were shuttered and doors closed. None of the companions had any desire to stay at another inn, so
they passed through each town at a steady trot.
For four more nights they camped in the woods,
taking care to conceal themselves from the road

as, each evening, they located a clearing near the bank of the mighty river.

Even as they drew closer to Vanderton, they saw few travelers. An occasional farmer took livestock to a village market, and infrequent fishers plied their nets in the placid river. Early on their last day, the riders passed the road leading to Oxvale, but Holt felt too much urgency to make a side trip to his home—it would mean the difference between seeing Danis late this afternoon, or not until the middle of the night. He looked at the green, pastoral hills, thought of the Jaken farmstead, and silently hoped his father would forgive him. Then, with apprehensions of Danis's peril as fresh as they had been when the hawk shrilled, he urged Old Thunder to greater speed.

As they drew near to Vanderton they came up behind a large, heavily laden wagon. A canvas tarp covered the bulging compartment and blocked their view of the occupants, and the huge wagon wheels fully straddled the road.

Old Thunder trotted easily through the ditch, passing the four-wheeled conveyance, which was pulled by two horses. These animals were big, strapping steeds, though not quite so large as the Daryman's own mount. Only when he pulled even with the driver's seat did he get the real surprise.

"Father!" Holt gasped, recognizing Derek Jaken smiling down from his high perch.

"Holton, my boy! This is a fortunate and welcome

meeting, indeed! Nowell, Hag, and I are on our way to Vanderton, to bring another load of the royal cheese."

Beside the farmer, beaming her toothless grin, was the elderly Hag Biddlesome, and beyond her, Nowell the Aching waved halfheartedly.

"I swear, this thing's going to rattle my bones to pieces!" groused Nowell, Holt's lifelong neighbor, shifting with obvious discomfort on the wagon's high seat. "Still, it's good to see you—and to know you survived a winter in the mountains. I shiver just to think about it!"

"But the wagon . . . ?" Holt was amazed by his father's mode of transport. The Jakens owned a two-wheeled cart, which Old Thunder had typically hauled to the city with loads of Oxvale's prized cheese. Since Derek had lost both his legs in battle many years earlier, he had depended on his son to do the transporting. Now, however, the elder Jaken sat comfortably on a padded bench, holding the reins and easily guiding the team along.

"The king liked the Oxvale cheeses so much, he gave this wagon to us—to the whole village. He sent the horses along in the bargain! His Majesty wants us to make regular deliveries of cheese, and he pays top price. There'll be no more long days of bartering in the marketplace."

Holt shook his head in amazement as Fenrald and Syssal greeted the Daryfolk. "The royal cheese, huh?" the dwarf mused. "Not surprising, really—I always told the lad here that the one thing humans do better than anyone else is make food!"

"I–I'm sorry I wasn't there to make the trip," Holt said, imagining the effect his half-year's stay in Graywall must have had on his father.

"Oh, don't trouble yourself," Derek said breezily. "Why, getting to Vanderton last fall reminded me how nice it is to see the countryside—and the city. I wouldn't have missed the trip. And Nowell's been having less trouble with his back. He was able to help out a lot more over the winter."

"Now it's my knees that are starting to go," Nowell said dejectedly. "I can hardly walk from my house to yours without limping!"

To Holt's considerable relief, this sounded pretty much like normal. Indeed, his father's expression seemed heartier, more vital than he ever remembered. Then Derek's eyebrows tucked into a frown, and he looked at Holt quizzically. "But what is it that brings *you* back to the city?"

"I . . . I have to see the First Daughter again," Holt declared vaguely, not wanting to share his own alarm with his father.

Thankfully, they had reached the long bridge leading to Vanderton, and when the riders preceded the wagon across the one-lane span, further conversation was stilled. The great river churned through a deep, stone-walled gorge below them, the city walls and green hills rising from the far bank.

Holt couldn't tear his eyes from the lofty castle before them. Tall, graceful towers challenged the sky, and an alabaster keep gleamed in the sunlight. Smooth walls of white stone rose from the crest of the city's highest hill, and three colorful pennants trailed from the topmost towers.

The small party made its way into the city, through streets bustling with the pushcarts of merchants and traders. Up the cobbled road they went, to the very gates of Castle Vanderthan.

On all sides, vendors hawked food and trinkets, smoke from smithies wafted through the street, and the hammering of busy carpenters resounded from many directions. Close to the castle, several companies of armed men marched a circuit through the streets, and Holt frowned at the implications of the unusual martial display.

Finally they reached the castle gates. Here, too, the guards waved them readily into the courtyard—quite a change from his first visit, Holt reflected, when he had had to trick his way past the guardhouse just to get a few words with the princess. From the courtyard, he saw that the battlements were manned by many guards. Above the lofty wall, he noticed hundreds of pigeons wheeling about the high towers, coming to rest on ramparts and flagpoles.

Before the stables, the travelers were met by a familiar figure, who bustled from the keep to greet them. Though he was little more than three feet tall, Gazzrick Whiptoe looked like a relieved grandfather as he trundled toward them. The halfling's long sideburns quivered, and his face beamed with a smile that could not quite overcome the concern in his large, dark eyes.

"I'm glad you're here!" Gazzrick said breathlessly as Holt, Fenrald, and Syssal dismounted.

The Daryman heartily clasped his diminutive friend by the hand, but looking into his eyes, Holt knew the halfling was deeply troubled.

"How is Danis?" he asked.

"She's frightened—but well. I'll take you to her in a moment."

Holt wanted to race through the doors of the castle, calling out the First Daughter's name. It was all he could do to remain patient as Gazzrick saw to the needs of his father and the other visitors from Oxvale.

Finally the halfling turned back to the young Daryman, the elf, and dwarf.

"Danis is with the king. They're having a . . . discussion, you could say. Yes, that's it—a somewhat *heated* discussion."

Holt couldn't suppress a tight smile. Danis was as strong-willed as her father, and neither the princess nor the king was likely to yield much ground in a "heated discussion."

"What are they talking about?" Syssal Kipican asked seriously.

"Dangers to the crown, and to the princess herself. As to how the artifact can best be protected."

"It makes sense to prepare the defenses, to keep the enemy outside the castle," Fenrald noted.

"It does—if the crown remains here," the halfling replied. "And the king feels the castle is the safest place for it."

"But Danis . . . ?" Holt could imagine the young woman's frustration with idle waiting, though his initial reaction was that her father was right.

"Danis is hoping you will all help her. She has a different idea."

"What?"

"She wants to take the crown, to journey with it to Tellist Tizzit's laboratory. She thinks there's only one way this problem will be solved, and Danis hopes he can give her advice."

Holt fondly remembered Tellist, the elderly wizard who had long been a friend of the Vanderthan family. Though prone to absentmindedness, the mage could cast a variety of powerful spells, and was surprisingly knowledgeable about matters arcane and historical.

"Advice about *what?*" demanded the dwarf.

Gazzrick sighed, and shook his head sadly. Finally, the royal advisor explained. "The First Daughter hopes Tellist Tizzit can figure out a way the Crown of Vanderthan can be destroyed. Danis feels that only when the artifact is gone will the kingdom be safe."

"Can't you call him here—with the chimes of summoning he gave you?"

"Er, the chimes have suffered a sort of malfunction," Gazzrick explained. "They still ring and so forth, but instead of bringing the wizard they seem to have provided a beacon to every pigeon within a hundred miles. We used them yesterday, as a matter of fact, and you can see what happened."

Laughing, the Daryman and his companions looked at the massive flock winging around the high towers. Many hundreds—perhaps a thousand or more—of the birds clustered around windows, perched on flagpoles, fluttered in agitation as the numerous guards shooed them from the upper battlements.

"And, speaking of birds, the carrier pigeons we've sent to him—and two mounted messengers—have never returned," Gazzrick said sadly. "Entropy is truly abroad in the lands."

"Holt!"

Her voice came from a gap in the garden hedge, and all of the Daryman's other thoughts flitted away.

"Danis!" he cried, leaping to his feet.

She ran toward him and his heart swelled with joy. The First Daughter's green eyes were shining, and her golden hair streamed behind like a shimmering wave of tangible sunlight. In the twilight, her smile was the brightest thing in Holt's world, and he grinned like a fool.

Immortal Game

All of his memories of that perfect face didn't do justice to the princess's true beauty. Holt held out his arms, wanting to embrace, to kiss and hold her, blocking out her fears and concerns and everything else. Only at the last moment did he recall the impervious barrier that would always exist between them.

Instead of clasping her, he took both of her hands in his and dropped to one knee. "Princess—my sword, my life are yours! You have but to command—"

"Oh, don't!" she declared, pulling him up by his hands and hugging him—an embrace he returned with a fervor that surprised him. For a moment, he melted into an exhilarated sense of happiness, while Danis looked over his shoulder at his companions. "And Fenrald, Syssal—my friends, it's so *good* to see you again."

"Ahem." The polite cough signalled the arrival of King Dathwell Vanderthan. Holt felt acutely uncomfortable, locked as he was in the arms of the monarch's daughter, but Danis wasn't quite ready to let go. Finally she released her grip, but still clutched his arm with both hands as she led him to her father.

"Your Majesty," Holt said with a bow. "It's good to see you again."

"See *me?*" Dathwell's words were light, but a stern glint filled his eye as he looked at his smiling, teary-eyed daughter. The monarch greeted the elf and the dwarf warmly, and Holt managed to pull free from Danis's hand—though it nearly broke his heart to do so. At least then he could stand before the king's gaze without squirming nervously.

"In truth, I am glad to see you, Daryman—and your bold companions, as well. You are welcome visitors in this time of disturbing portent."

"You, too, received a warning?" Holt asked.

"One that was so unnatural it couldn't be ignored. It was my hound—he *spoke* to me, I swear, speaking the name of my daughter and the word *crown*."

"It was a hawk who spoke the same to Fenrald and myself—we came as quickly as we could, fearing the princess was in peril," Holt replied sincerely.

"Stop saying that!" Danis snapped, surprising Holt—who to the best of his memory had not previously said anything of the kind. "I mean, that's just what my father has been going on about—that *I'm* in some kind of danger!"

"My dear, there's no doubt in my mind that this onslaught of evil is directed at you! You must take precautions, be protected—"

"And what about the rest of you?" Danis demanded, her hands on her hips. She glared belligerently at Holt. "So *you,* too, heard about my being in danger?"

He nodded grimly. "From the hawk, yes," he

repeated.

"Don't you see—it's not me that they're after—it's the Crown of Vanderthan!"

"Now I don't concede that for a minute," the king said firmly. "But even if I did, it would be madness to carry the artifact off from the castle on some quest to have it destroyed! It's safe where it is—as safe as it can be!"

"And there's another thing," Holt agreed. "We don't even know if it *can* be destroyed."

"It can," Danis said firmly.

"I tried, once, to get rid of it," the Daryman reminded her. "But the wind blew it back, snagged it on the cliff—"

"And a good thing it did. No, we can't just throw it away. Down the precipice of World's End, deep in the ocean—wherever it would end up, there'd be a chance some creature of Entropy would be able to reach it. That would be just like handing it over—no, we've got to destroy it."

"But *how?*" Holt persisted.

"Tellist Tizzit would be able to figure out a way."

"I told you—it's safe, here," the king interjected. "If you go trundling it across the countryside, who knows what fiends of Entropy might be waiting to ambush you on the trail?"

"If we *don't* get it out of here, those same fiends are going to come into the castle and get it!" Danis argued. "Think of *that*—Vanderton razed, Castle Vanderthan breached! It could mean the end of the kingdom!"

"It told you—it's *safe* here!"

"Your Majesty?" Syssal Kipican inquired politely. "I've had a little experience in the protection and, er, acquisition of valuables. It's been my discovery that *nothing* is as safely kept as its owner imagines. Perhaps we could inspect the crown's current defenses, at least to evaluate their possible improvement."

"Splendid idea," King Dathwell agreed readily. "Fits right in with my thinking—that the crown should stay just where it is."

Without hesitation, the monarch and Danis led Holt, Syssal, and Fenrald into a side door of the keep. Full night had fallen, and as they passed the kitchen, scents of garlic, baking bread, and roasting poultry teased their nostrils. The king ignored the tempting smells, pushing on to stop beside a door where two men-at-arms stood on duty. They saluted as he opened the heavy portal and started down a long, musty stairway of stone.

The descent was lighted only by an occasional flickering torch, but the group continued for a good distance underground. At the foot of the long flight of steps, the king unlocked a barred door, took one of the torches, and led the others along a dark and narrow passageway.

"I keep a guard outside the treasure room at all times," Dathwell proclaimed, raising the torch over his head to reveal the vague outlines of a dark, solid-looking door. "It's just along here—

"By the Spheres! What happened!"

The monarch shouted in surprise and started forward, toward a locked, barred door. A shadowy object lay in a crumple before it.

Lodestone Blade in hand, the Daryman pushed past the king and knelt beside the collapsed form, recognizing the tunic of a castle guardsman. Even before he touched the pallid, chilly skin, Holt knew the fellow was dead.

The torch shaking in his hand, King Dathwell lowered the blazing brand toward the man's face. "It's Rogarick! But I'd hardly know him—he seems so shriveled, wasted!"

Holt saw a pair of tiny wounds on the man's neck, punctures barely an inch or two apart. Blood, still fresh, trickled from the spots. A quick glance showed no other sign of injury.

"The door!" Syssal said urgently. "Open it!"

"Well, yes," the king stammered. "But you can see that it's still locked. Whoever killed Rogarick couldn't have gotten in—I have the only key!"

"Open it!" hissed the elf.

His hand still shaking, Dathwell fumbled with a large iron ring. He found a key and managed to insert it. The lock released with a grinding creak.

As soon as the door began to move, Holt and Fenrald pushed it open and charged into the room. The torch remained outside, but the gentle glow of magic immediately revealed that the Crown of

38

Vanderthan was still there, resting upon a block of stone. Three heavy chains were linked through the crown, then anchored to massive bolts driven into the rock.

Only then did Holt notice the other, shadowy occupant of the room. So dark was the intruder that at first the Daryman had just seen a patch of blackness beyond the crown. But when that darkness moved, the Daryman cried out in shock and fear.

The figure was manlike, but larger than life. It wore a black cloak that extended like a huge wing when its long, skeletal arms were raised. Its face was ghostly white, except for the twin trickles of blood that still gleamed on the pale chin. Two furious spots of flaming ember were its eyes.

"*Vampire!*" gasped Fenrald, raising his hammer menacingly.

Holt wielded his own blade before his face, as if trying to ward off the pure evil in the creature's hateful gaze. The orbs in the pale face flashed, as red as bloodstains, and the Daryman felt a piercing, paralyzing terror. Vaguely, he saw the thing's clawlike hands grasp one of the chains binding the crown. With barely a visible effort, the creature snapped the heavy iron links.

"Stop!" King Dathwell stepped past Holt, but the monster's eyes flashed again, and the monarch sank to the floor with a groan.

Before the others could move, those eyes flamed

again, and Holt's body—his will—was no longer his own. Grimly, but without hurrying, the creature seized and snapped the second of the three chains.

The Daryman strained to break the grip of the paralysis, to move a leg or bend an arm, but his feet might have been glued to the floor.

The third chain snapped, and Danis screamed, her voice ringing through the small, stone-walled chamber. The terror audible in that sound electrified Holt, broke the spell of numbness that encased him.

Leaping forward, he saw the monster touch the crown with one skeletal hand. The Lodestone Blade whistled through the air, then met the bony wrist of the monster. Holt slashed through and raised the weapon again, watching as the crown— still clutched by the severed, clawlike appendage— dropped back to its rocky pedestal.

The one-handed creature stumbled away from the artifact. The vampire's mouth gaped, and the Daryman saw vicious fangs, heard the hissing of the monster's fury. Shouting with rage of his own, Holt lunged. The hideous bloodsucker feared the Lodestone Blade—and it had very rarely feared anything before. The thick stench of the beast's breath washed over Holt, reeking like a freshly opened crypt, gagging him with its putrid foulness. The Daryman slashed again, and the monster leapt away, retreating into a corner. Holt charged recklessly, wanting nothing more than to hack the horrifying and deadly thing to bits—

But it was no longer there.

A cloud of vile mist *whooshed* through the air, swirling out of the corner as the Daryman chopped and stabbed with his sword, meeting no resistance. The greenish cloud circled around, and again Holt caught the scent of rot . . . and worse.

"There it goes!"

Danis clasped her hands to her head and screamed as the gust swirled through her hair. The torch sputtered in the hallway, then flared, and the companions heard the moaning of wind along the passageway, sweeping toward the world outside.

3
To End an Artifact

King Dathwell groaned weakly, and Danis helped him sit up.

"The crown. . . ? There, I see it," he muttered weakly. "By the Spheres of Darkness—what *was* that thing?"

"The news could hardly be more dire, Your Majesty," Syssal Kipican declared slowly. "That horror was a vampire, one of the most potent of the undead. It's a creature of the night, a rapacious taker of life."

"I've never heard of such a creature—why is it

abroad now?" demanded the king.

"The twin corruptions of werewolf and vampire are both visited upon Karawenn. It can only mean that the forces of Entropy are very determined, indeed. Our enemies apparently have a plan—masterminded by some foul thing." The elf spoke with grim certainty.

"And it came for the *crown,* not for me!" declared Danis triumphantly. "That proves it—we have to destroy the artifact!"

"But—the key?" The monarch gestured at the heavy door. "How did it get through the locks?"

"Same way it flew out," Fenrald observed. "Turned itself into a cloud of mist. Probably floated right under the door—after it killed your man."

"Poor Rogarick—a brave and loyal swordsman, he was," the king said sadly. "And alert, too—I wonder how the beast took him so quietly?"

"He never had a chance, Your Majesty," Syssal noted. "The eyes of the vampire can root a victim to the ground, holding him helpless to react."

"I felt the same thing," Holt said.

"Rogarick will get the full honors of a warrior's burial," pledged the king, clearly moved—and frightened.

Danis lifted the crown and held it in her hands. She looked at her father, her eyes sympathetic but her words firm. "The crown is *not* safe in the castle. I have the bravest friends in all Karawenn to protect me—let me take it to the wizard, to seek his advice! He may have a spell, know some mixture of alchemy, that will allow him to destroy it!"

Dathwell looked at the stout door, then let his eyes linger on the body of his loyal guardsman. Finally, he turned to examine the three chains, each of which had been snapped like string by the horrific intruder.

"Sire, that vampire's still alive," Holt noted. "We have to expect it'll be back. And I think the princess is right—the crown has to be destroyed. Surely Tellist Tizzit is our best bet to find a way."

The monarch seemed smaller than he had before. He regarded the circlet of silvery metal in his daughter's hands. Then, sighing in resignation, he nodded.

"It shall be as you wish—with one condition."

"What?" the princess asked suspiciously.

"Try to destroy it here first—fire the smithy, do anything you can to see if the cursed thing can be melted down or smashed to pieces!"

"Good idea," Fenrald said, flexing his hammering arm. "Let's get some coal burning and see what we can do."

Danis and the king led them to the blacksmith's shop, which was a shed near the stable. Fenrald donned a leather apron, heavy gauntlets, and a screen-mesh mask. He stoked the furnace until the blaze roared, the cast iron glowing cherry red and spewing clouds of smoke. Yet when he tossed the crown in atop the furiously burning coals, it remained unscathed. The dwarf worked the bellows until his own lungs were blowing as hard as the big fan, but even as the walls of the forge glowed yellow, the platinum circlet sat unaffected by the heat.

Removing the artifact with the smith's tongs, the dwarf set it upon the anvil and hefted the heavy hammer. Repeated blows set their ears to ringing, but had no effect on the crown. Cursing, Fenrald hoisted the mallet with both hands, the sinews in his arms standing out like taut cords as he brought it down for one final smash. That blow did result in destruction—of the hammer, which snapped off at the base of the head and went *zinging* across the shop, nearly striking the king himself. Still there was no mark on the sparkling, gem-studded circlet.

Finally Fenrald hefted his own warhammer in his hand. Holt watched anxiously, knowing how the dwarf treasured the enchanted weapon—which would magically return to his hand when he threw it against an opponent. Now Fenrald brought that heavy steel head smashing down on the frail-looking artifact. Metallic clashes rang through the shop, and sparks flew from the anvil, obscuring the crown and the pounding hammer in a haze of smoke and brightness. Finally the dwarf stumbled backward, gasping for breath, and the smoke wafted through the open doors of the shed.

The crown still rested on the anvil, unscratched,

unmelted, and apparently indestructible.

Holt began to wonder if even the wizard Tellist Tizzit would know how the crown could be destroyed. As dawn streaked the sky beyond the castle walls and the fires in the forge slowly settled to coals, he knew they would have to try.

The companions, smoke-stained and smudged, emerged into the crisp air of the courtyard. The princess turned a faint smile toward her father.

"*Now* you have to let us go," she said smugly.

With a pained sigh, the king nodded. "I fear terribly for you," he said, his voice catching. "But you're right—there's no good alternative."

"I'll be safe, Father—you know that!" Danis declared with forced enthusiasm. Obviously the monarch's worry touched her more deeply than she wanted to admit. The First Daughter insisted they depart by noon, so the company dispersed to get a few hours' sleep.

Despite his short rest, Holt had no trouble waking up. He was invigorated by the prospects of a ride—at least, a ride in the company of Danis Vanderthan. The Daryman dressed quickly, and gathered his few personal items in his backpack.

He started across the courtyard to the stables, but was surprised when King Dathwell fell into step beside him. Before they reached the doors to the keep, the monarch paused and touched the Daryman on the arm. To Holt he looked no longer regal, but fatherly—and frightened.

"If—if anything happens to her, I don't think that the queen would be able to cope with the tragedy," Dathwell declared hesitantly, looking at the ground. Abruptly his eyes met Holt's, and the Daryman saw the dire worry there. "Nor, I suppose, could I. You understand that, don't you?"

"Sire—I would lay down my life for her!" It was the truth, and spoken without regret. Dathwell's fear touched Holt, but still he could not banish a pang of resentment: the king would never consent to have his daughter marry a commoner, though he took it for granted that the Daryman would be willing to die for her.

The very real prospects of danger quickly overwhelmed Holt's momentary irritation. He vowed privately to do everything in his power to see that their quest was a success, and that Danis came through the experience without harm.

"I've never doubted your courage, or your loyalty," the king replied, speaking hesitantly—but forging ahead with determination. "See here, lad—if the circumstances of the past, of birth and station, could be in any way altered, I would do so. But we both know that's impossible."

Dathwell stopped walking, turning to face Holt squarely. The king's expression became stern, but then softened into the anxiety the Daryman had noticed moments before. "I'm not so blind to overlook the strength of your affections—nor am I unaware that they are fully reciprocated by the

First Daughter. I can only confess my faith in your steadfastness during a painful and difficult time."

Holt's silence seemed to make the king a trifle uneasy. After a moment, however, the Daryman chided himself for his petulance—the menace that was the Crown of Vanderthan far outweighed the importance of his own selfish desires.

"We'll travel with all speed," he assured the king. "If Tellist can give us some help, I don't doubt the First Daughter will be back home safely in a week or so."

"Yes—that's all we can hope for, isn't it?"

Neither the king nor Holt spoke of the other, darker fear that lurked in their thoughts: what if Tellist Tizzit *didn't* know a way that the crown could be destroyed? That was a possibility the young Daryman, for his part, refused even to contemplate.

"Holt! Don't you have Old Thunder saddled yet?" Danis chided, coming out of the keep to find the two men ending their conversation. "The afternoon will slip away on us!"

He hurried to the stables, thankful when Fenrald tromped from the castle, carrying both his own and Holt's gear. Neither of them had a large saddlebag, and they were quickly mounted and ready to ride. Danis, astride her eager black charger, Lancer, awaited them in the courtyard. The Crown of Vanderthan had been rolled into the First Daughter's bedroll, secured behind the saddle. Syssal was there too, mounted on a small but fleet gray mare.

"I'm coming, too." They turned to see Gazzrick Whiptoe leading his shaggy pony—a mount similar to Fenrald's—from another stall in the stable.

"Oh, Gazzrick—thank you," Danis said. "But don't you think you'd serve better at father's side? You know how he depends on you."

"Posh and nonsense! I can still mount a horse—well, a pony, anyway. I can see, and I know how to hold a sword. I don't see how you can turn me down!"

She tried to dissuade him, but the halfling stubbornly mounted and trotted along with the companions as they started toward the castle gates. It was a party of five that clattered through the streets of Vanderton and soon cantered along the highway between the brown, freshly tilled fields of spring. A musty, fertile scent rose from the ground, filling the Daryman with a growing sense of hope and vitality.

"Where do we find Tellist?" Holt asked. Always before, the wizard had magically teleported himself to the castle.

"I've been to his house—it's more of a laboratory, actually," Danis said. "He lives in the Rocklands, along a ridge he calls Stone Bank. It's about three days' ride."

"I think it would be best to avoid inns and villages, as much as possible," Syssal suggested.

"Both because the threats of Entropy can easily go disguised among men, and because the crown would bring danger among the innocent."

"Good idea," Danis agreed, and Holt nodded in silent approval. Their shocking encounter in the Catfish Inn was still fresh in his mind. He knew their chances of defending themselves were better when they didn't have to worry about other distractions.

They rode as quickly as the horses' stamina would allow, sometimes cantering, frequently trotting, then slowing to a steady walk to allow the lathered steeds to regain their wind. At dusk they saw lights twinkling in a small village to their right, but none of the companions suggested they seek indoor shelter. Instead, they rode for a few more miles and discovered a mossy meadow near a shallow, splashing brook.

"Let's take turns standing watch," Holt suggested.

"Aye—we should have two of us awake at all times," Fenrald said. "And whoever's up—be sure to keep your eyes open!"

After a cold dinner of cheese, bread, and jerky, they stretched their bedrolls under the shelter of widespread oak limbs. "I'll take the first shift," Holt offered.

"I'll join you," Gazzrick announced. "My backside's still too sore for lying on the ground, anyway."

"Princess, why don't you sleep with the crown beside you?" Syssal suggested. "Fenrald and I can take the watch from midnight till dawn."

Danis objected, but the four of them convinced her that the crown would be better protected this way. Shortly after dark, exhausted by the long, hard trek, Danis, Fenrald, and Syssal had drifted off to sleep. Holt and Gazzrick paced slowly around the periphery of their small camp, eyes trying to penetrate the darkness.

Did werewolves lurk in those shadows? Or perhaps the vampire? Holt remembered the awful visage of that undead horror, and he began to imagine the flash of those red eyes every time he turned around. Night settled around him in shadows thicker than any he had ever seen.

"It's getting cold, don't you think?" Gazzrick asked, materializing from the mist, shivering though his cloak was pulled all the way over his head.

"Cold . . . and quiet," Holt observed. Even the insects, which had been coming to life all across Karawenn during the advancing spring, now seemed reluctant to break the stillness of the night.

Holt stiffened, seeing movement in the shadows. He relaxed as he recognized a bush, swaying in the gentle breeze. As the night wore on, though, he felt increasingly jumpy, often whirling quickly with the sensation that something was sneaking up behind him.

Even so, when he turned and saw the crimson, hateful eyes boring out of the darkness, stark terror jolted through him with numbing force. Like twin beacons of ravenous horror, the fiery orbs transfixed him from the woods just beyond the camp.

The Daryman's lips strained to make a sound, to shout the alarm that would draw Gazzrick's attention and awaken his companions. Holt's hand groped toward the hilt of the Lodestone Blade, but he felt mired, as if his entire body were encased in thick mud.

The vampire approached, swirling out of the darkness with movement too fluid for walking—the creature seemed to glide over the ground, the black cloak floating behind it. The red eyes grew from spots to narrow, slitted ovals of evil, burning with hatred . . . and hunger. Holt had a vivid memory of the unfortunate guard in Castle Vanderthan, the body drained of blood, the shriveled, pathetic corpse left behind.

But still he couldn't force himself to move, to make a sound. The hateful orbs bored into his face, paralyzing him with mind-numbing fear. Now he saw the vampire's pale, ghastly skin, the glistening fangs revealed when horrific jaws opened wide. A tongue, slick and wet and red as fresh blood, flickered between the monster's cruel fangs.

The two arms reached forward, and a dim portion

of Holt's mind saw that one of the black sleeves was empty, where the hand had been severed by the Lodestone Blade. The other, a bent and crooked claw, reached toward the Daryman's chest. Fearing his heart could be torn from his rib cage, Holt strained desperately to break the thrall—but he could only watch with despairing, horrified fascination as the blood-red fingernails approached his tunic.

Something tumbled past his legs, and Holt staggered backward, shaking his head as if awakening from a vivid nightmare. Gazzrick!

The halfling's sword jabbed against the vampire's belly, bouncing off the monster's skin. Gazzrick leapt in with surprising agility, reaching, seizing the vampire's arm. With a wrenching, downward twist, the diminutive fellow pulled, yanking the monster off balance.

"Wake up! It's *here!*" cried Holt, finally drawing his sword. The blade glowed with a vengeful light, and the vampire raised its handless arm to ward its eyes against the glow. At the same time, the monster twisted its wicked claw, seizing Gazzrick around the neck and shaking him like a rag doll.

Fenrald, Syssal, and Danis scrambled to their feet, instantly awake and armed.

Holt heard pathetic wails from somewhere nearby and dimly realized Gazzrick was groaning weakly in the vampire's grasp. The Daryman lunged, but the monster tossed the halfling toward him. Swinging his blade to the side, Holt caught Gazzrick in his free hand and gently lowered him to the ground. Even as he turned toward the beast, Holt was appalled by the deadly chill he felt in the halfling's motionless body.

"Look out!" screamed the princess, her words jerking Holt's attention upward.

The vampire pounced like a panther, cape streaming behind, jaws straining toward the Daryman. Holt raised his sword instinctively, driving the gray, stony blade upward as he tried to screen Gazzrick's body with his own.

Foul breath washed over him in a thick cloud of stench. Retching, the Daryman held his sword arm firm, feeling the weight of the hideous creature smashing against the blade. The stone tip pierced the vampire's chest, and as Holt tumbled backward, borne down by the beast's weight, he heard its otherworldly scream of anguish.

Desperately, he pushed at the hideous form, revolted by the touch of the cold flesh. He pulled free his weapon and raised the Lodestone Blade again as the monster tumbled to the side.

"Hold," said Fenrald firmly, and only then did Holt realize he was trembling with fury. He had hacked the monster's head from its shoulders, then mindlessly raised his weapon for another blow, but the dwarf's calming word brought him back to reality.

"The beast is dead," Syssal said, kneeling beside

the gruesome form. "There are not many things that will slay such as he. Your sword is mighty, indeed," the elf said with a nod toward Holt.

"Gazzrick?" gasped the Daryman, kneeling beside Danis as the princess examined the halfling. "Does he live?"

"He's weak, but alive," the princess said.

"He saved my life—saved us all!" Holt cried, his voice choking from shame. "I saw the creature coming, but I was helpless to move, even to speak. I–I just *stood* there, waiting! Gazzrick threw himself at the vampire when it was about to kill me."

"Let it never be said that size is a measure of courage," the elf said somberly, kneeling beside the motionless halfling. Syssal looked up. "Nor is paralysis in the face of a vampire any cause for shame. Any one of us, should we have met its eyes, would have been doomed."

Gazzrick coughed suddenly, and then his teeth began to chatter.

Danis wrapped him in a robe and held him tight. For the rest of the night, she kept him bundled under all the blankets they had. With the dawn, the halfling's face was pale, his skin pasty, but his eyes were open. He smiled weakly at Holt, and it was the finest smile the Daryman had ever seen.

"We got the thing, right?" he asked.

"Aye, old friend—thanks to you," Holt said.

Teeth still chattering, Gazzrick closed his eyes.

Shudders racked his body, and he couldn't stop shivering.

"We've got to get him to shelter, to a bed," declared Danis.

"Wha . . . ? *No*." The halfling's protests were mumbled from the depths of his misery.

Despite his protestations, Gazzrick was obviously injured too badly to continue the ride. After a few minutes of agonized discussion, the companions decided to take him back to the village they had passed before finding their campsite. Holt held Gazzrick before him on Old Thunder, and they quickly made their way to the small community. At the outskirts, they met a farmer who was taking a load of eggs and poultry to Vanderton, and he promised to carry word to the king—who would undoubtedly send a wagon to carry the halfling back to the castle. Soon, they had the local innkeeper fully impressed by the royal credentials of his guest.

"I still say I can ride!" insisted Gazzrick, snuggled beneath the quilts in the best room of the village's only inn. A fire blazed in a hearth beside the bed, and the halfling had finally stopped shivering.

"I know you can," Holt said, blinking back his tears as he looked at his friend's wan expression. "It's just that—I don't think the rest of us could keep up!"

Gazzrick was still chuckling as Holt closed the door and went to the street. He looked backward several times while the four companions mounted up. Then they started once more along the trail to the Rocklands.

4
The House of Tellist Tizzit

The riders pressed forward, but without spirit
or enthusiasm. The loss of the halfling had affected
them each in a deep, uncanny way. Holt's eyes
scanned each tree, every clump of brush beside the
trail; any of the landmarks could conceal brutal
ambushers. Syssal, too, scrutinized the woodlands
alertly, while Danis sat dejectedly in her saddle,
staring at little beyond Lancer's mane. Fenrald, in
his customary position at the rear, often halted
and hid himself, checking against pursuit and then
galloping his pony into a lather in his haste to

catch up with his companions.

They entered a desolate woodland. Numerous dead trees jutted like skeletal spikes from the ground. An odor of rot and decay rose from many puddles of stagnant water, and once the party stumbled upon the half-decayed body of a deer— long dead, but without visible wounds.

"Entropy's everywhere around here," Holt muttered bitterly, pulling his collar over his mouth in a futile effort to stifle the stench of the carrion.

"You're right . . . never have I seen a woodland so utterly devoid of life." Syssal Kipican's expression remained calm, but the depths of his anguish showed in the elf's emerald eyes.

Danis sighed heavily. "It's as if this whole part of Karawenn is dying. Entropy is eating the world away, so to speak."

"I say—here's a patch of gloomy travelers! And it's not even raining!" The familiar voice emerged from the branches of a nearby tree.

"Sir Ira!" Danis cried.

Holt brightened immediately, looking upward to see the barrel-shaped body of an owl. The bird blinked sagely before spreading his broad wings and gliding down to light on the First Daughter's saddle.

"A bit far from home, aren't we?" he inquired. Still riding, the companions filled him in on the nature of their mission.

"Werewolves? Vampires? That explains some of

the howling I've heard at night—and a few of the darker shadows moving through the woods." The owl frowned thoughtfully and took a moment to ponder the predicament. The others waited patiently—they all had good reason to remember and respect the wise old bird's knowledge and judgment. "All told, I'd say destroying the crown is a good idea!"

"We don't even know if Tellist can do it," Danis said. "We're trying to get to his house as fast as possible."

"Why don't I fly ahead to alert him—perhaps he can teleport out to meet you, or something."

"That's a great idea," the princess replied, but then she shook her head thoughtfully. "Still, I've known Tellist to teleport himself to . . . the wrong place, sometimes."

"I take your point," the owl agreed. Indeed, they were all familiar with the well-meaning wizard's magic powers—which did not always have the effect Tellist desired.

Danis made a suggestion. "Perhaps it would be better if he stayed put and made some preparations—so that when we got there with the crown he could get right to work."

"Righto! I'm off to Stone Bank!" With a nod of his tufted head, Sir Ira took wing and quickly dwindled to a speck in the sky.

The other companions, significantly more hopeful than they had been in the morning, rode rapidly for the rest of the day. Sir Ira Hsiao was not only wise, but also gifted in magical powers of healing, and if the quest so far was any indication, they'd be needing a healer.

The riders spent that night, and the next, camping watchfully, but suffered no additional nocturnal attacks—nor did they encounter difficulty on the trail. On the third morning, they rode urgently, entering the Rocklands, expecting to catch sight of Stone Bank beyond each bend of the path.

"We're getting close," Danis observed, pointing to a lion-shaped crest of granite thrusting upward from the forest. "That promontory is visible from Tellist's house."

The companions made their way around the boulder-strewn outcrop, noting that the trail narrowed and began to climb. Abruptly, they came to a wide field of clover with a flat-faced bluff rising beyond. A waterfall trilled musically down the surface of that cliff, splashing into a clear, deep pool. Flowers blossomed in abundance, and Holt watched with delight as several of the lush petals faded through a rainbow assortment of colors, changing before his eyes!

Thick evergreens crowded shoulder to shoulder along the base of the bluff, and the Daryman could see no sign of a house. He did spot a massive wooden door that was apparently set right into the wall of Stone Bank, and when he got a better look, he saw that the gargantuan entrance was flanked by twin statues of fierce-looking monsters.

"Drat! Confound it! You contemptuous nag!"

A burst of shouts erupted from a nearby cluster of pines. The reedy voice, shrill with irritation, could only belong to the wizard.

"This is Tellist's stable," Danis explained, leading the other riders between several feathered evergreens. Holt inhaled deeply, relishing the lush scent of pine.

They quickly discovered the bedraggled figure of Tellist Tizzit beside a lanky horse. The bearded old wizard was shouting, shaking his fists at the nag's ears, tugging on the reins—but the animal was contentedly grazing on the long green grass and the lush, flowering clover that flourished among the trees.

"Tellist!" cried Danis, dismounting and rushing to give the wizard a hug.

His robe flapping, Tellist wrapped one arm around her while tugging at the reins with the other.

"Why, hello, my dear! Tut, tut, I wanted to be ready to ride when you got here. But Dragonfire's taste for clover is getting the better of me!"

The Daryman regarded the potbellied, sway-backed mare skeptically. If there was any horse *less* deserving of a name like Dragonfire, Holt had yet to see it. Still, the steed seemed somehow appropriate for the elderly wizard. Perhaps, like Tellist himself, the mount was not as frail as she appeared.

Sir Ira spiraled down to settle onto Lancer's saddle. "I gave him the message about your plans," the owl declared, frowning as Tellist's hand slipped from the reins and the elderly mage toppled to his hindquarters in the grass.

"And I'm glad you thought of me!" Tellist proclaimed, allowing Danis to help him to his feet. Then he blinked his watery eyes and peered through his metal-framed spectacles. "Sir Ira tells me you wish to destroy the crown—splendid idea, simply splendid. As I've said more than once, that artifact is nothing but trouble. Best gotten rid of, quickly."

"Then you can help us?" Danis asked.

"Why, my dear, of course I can . . . er, I could— and I would! Tut, tut—that is, I would if I could, but I'm afraid I don't have the foggiest notion of how one could go about destroying it."

With a groan, the princess slumped her shoulders. Holt felt a surge of frustration, followed quickly by despair. The problem wasn't Tellist's fault, but surely there must be *some* way to accomplish the task!

"Still, there's a few things we might try—alchemist's secrets, brews and formulae, the like. Perhaps you'll come with me to my laboratory?"

"Yes!" chimed Holt and Danis, while Fenrald and the elf nodded firm assent.

After unsaddling the horses and seeing that the

weary steeds had ample supplies of forage and water, the companions accompanied the wizard toward what appeared to be a looming, natural wall of stone. Only one feature looked artificial, the great oak door flanked by two glaring gargoyles. But when Holt started for the huge door, Tellist held up a hand.

"Tut, tut—that one's just for show. I wouldn't touch it if I were you. Wouldn't be nice, at all."

Gulping, the Daryman warily eyed the massive oaken barrier. The two statues stared, teeth bared menacingly. Tellist, meanwhile, pushed his way between the branches of a pair of thick evergreens. Beyond these lay a shadowy niche, between a pair of boulders. The aperture was screened by a thick clump of thorny brambles, and the Daryman couldn't fathom how anyone could pass there without having his skin ripped to shreds.

Astonishingly, Tellist stepped right into the thicket, and the wicked-looking branches vanished the instant the wizard touched them. The portal revealed was a wide arch, obviously formed by the efforts of a builder—or by magic. In any event, stout supporting pillars to either side and a smooth overhead lintel proved this was no naturally formed cave.

The travelers followed the wizard through the stone archway and into the soothing, cinnamon-scented air wafting coolly through the cavelike tunnel. The space was dark, but Holt could tell by the echoes of their footsteps that it was large.

"Tut, tut—perhaps some illumination would help," muttered the wizard. He spoke a sharp word, and many spots of light twinkled over his head.

The companions stood in a large room, with wood-paneled walls and heavy beams on the ceiling, illuminated by a crystal chandelier supporting dozens of candles. In the center of the space stood a long table of polished wood, resting on rugs of ornate weave. It was surrounded by hardwood chairs with plush velvet cushions. Through arched doorways, Holt caught sight of other rooms, all illuminated in tastefully dim candlelight.

"Through here—to the laboratory. Let's not waste time!" Tellist urged, ushering the companions through several more opulent chambers. The whole place would have done justice to a noble's manor, Holt thought. Finally they reached a large room with walls of white stone, and three massive windows providing views in different directions.

Expecting vistas of the Rocklands, Holt was shocked to see an azure ocean, a rugged mountain peak, and a lush forest broken by the expanse of a clear lake.

"Oh, they keep changing," Tellist declared, waving at the windows. Blinking, the Daryman missed a sudden transformation—but now the forest scene had been replaced by a brilliant swath of glacier, spilling in an alabaster floe from a low valley. Sunlight reflected from the snow so brightly that Holt squinted involuntarily. Then the room's other features caught his attention.

In the center of the laboratory stood a block of stone—a table as solid as any Holt had ever seen. Several large books, open to marked pages, each with numerous ribbons of bookmarks dangling from other passages, lay upon the table. The tomes were surrounded by an assortment of multicolored glass bottles and small wooden boxes with inlaid tops and tiny, intricate locks. A hand-sized charcoal brazier glowed at one end of the surface, beneath a black iron kettle that bubbled noisily and belched clouds of bluish, noxious steam.

The walls were lined with numerous shelves, all of which were crowded with more vials, books, bottles, and casks, and many more unidentifiable objects. Holt thought he recognized several dried bat's wings, but many other shapeless, dark objects mystified him. He thought, with a shudder, that it was perhaps better not to ask what they contained.

"Well, first the acid bath," declared the wizard.

Danis handed him the crown, and he lowered the artifact into the bubbling kettle. More steam belched forth, hissing and sputtering angrily. Holt's initial optimism was quelled several minutes later when Tellist reached into the caldron with a pair of tongs and lifted out the gem-studded artifact, still gleaming and undamaged.

Next the mage dusted the Crown of Vanderthan with powder before chanting an incantation that caused the dust to burst into flame. The blaze died quickly, once again leaving the crown unscathed.

"There's one other thing I can try—though I hesitate," declared the wizard, as the smoke cloud dissipated gradually.

"What's that?" Holt asked warily.

"Try it!" declared Danis, even before the wizard could answer.

"It's just that—tut, tut—the disintegrate spell is one of my most powerful. If anything should go wrong . . ."

"We don't have a choice." The princess was adamant. "If the crown can be destroyed, the effort is worth it!"

"Very well." With a few murmured *tut, tut*s, Tellist moved the books and vials aside and placed the crown in the center of his worktable. After urging the companions to stand against the far wall, he muttered the words to his spell, pointing a forefinger at the crown. The strange, chanting sounds built gradually to a resonant crescendo—in a voice that seemed too strong to emerge from the wizard's frail chest and skinny throat.

A resounding shock echoed through the lab, accompanied by tinkling glass as bottles fell from shelves. An acrid cloud of rock dust floated in the air, but as the debris settled, Holt saw with hope that the worktable was gone. In fact, a wide crater stood in the floor at the center of the room.

"Drat!" Tellist declared, looking into the pit and dashing the companions' hopes. Stepping to the wizard's side, Holt saw the platinum circlet gleaming amid a rubble of gravel. Dejectedly he slid into the hole, then crawled back out with the unscathed artifact in his hand.

"You mean it *can't* be destroyed?" demanded Danis, glowering at the crown as if she could melt it with the strength of her glare.

"I have a suggestion—a course of action you might be willing to consider," the mage said hesitantly. "After all, divining arcane truths—such as how to destroy artifacts—is not my specialty of magic. There are some, however, who are very skilled at the solving of this kind of mystery."

"Who?" the princess demanded.

"You remember Prince Gallarath, of course?"

"I'll never forget him," Danis replied—in a tone that Holt couldn't interpret, but that still caused him a flash of jealousy. Gallarath was the crown prince of Rochester, the realm beyond Vanderthan, and he had been the victor in a contest King Dathwell had arranged. Because of the prince's success, the king had offered Gallarath the First Daughter's hand in marriage—which Danis had refused, much to her father's displeasure. Gallarath had been a trustworthy and courageous companion, but still the Daryman could not help thinking of him as Danis's future husband.

"Well, he's King Gallarath now—his father passed away over the winter," Tellist continued, piquing Holt's curiosity and apprehension. "In any event, I've heard that he has a seer at his court—a fellow of some ability, according to rumor, able to predict the future, that sort of thing. Perhaps he could provide the kind of arcane help we need."

"Let's try it. How far to Rochester?" the princess asked quickly.

"Perhaps another two days—though I could teleport ahead, maybe save us—"

"No!" Danis declared.

"That is, we can ride quickly," the Daryman added. "Dragonfire will get that chance to run after all."

5
Gallarath

Their plans made, and Tellist with a bedroll and provisions already packed, the companions departed the Rocklands on the road to Rochester. Continuing to avoid inns and towns, they camped watchfully and rode hard. These were the nights of the waning moon, and though they maintained guards at all times, they encountered none of the horrible agents of Entropy.

Dragonfire proved quite capable of long hours on the trail, and the five riders and the owl came into sight of Gallarath's capital in late afternoon of the second day after departing Tellist's house.

Even from the outside, Holt could see that Rochester was a pale comparison to Vanderthan. The city was surrounded by a wooden palisade, and the few stone buildings jutting above the wall were square and blocky. He saw none of the soaring towers and elegant turrets that distinguished Dathwell's city.

The riders came through the city gates at a walk, joining the farmers and workers who thronged the crowded, narrow streets. Even the main thoroughfare was an avenue of dirt and mud—nowhere did Holt see cobblestones or paving bricks on the ground. Rats swarmed everywhere between the buildings, through the narrow and cluttered alleys. The scavengers were obviously bold enough to scurry about in broad daylight, in numbers greater than Holt had ever seen.

The castle was the largest structure in Rochester, consisting of a rough, cube-shaped keep encircled by another wooden palisade. Apparently word of their arrival had preceded them, for the castle gates were open and the guards ushered them inside. Prince—*King*, Holt reminded himself—Gallarath himself came out to meet them, flanked by his brother Wallas and a short man with a pointed nose and bright, bloodshot eyes.

"My princess! This is indeed an honor!" declared Gallarath, with what Holt took as forced heartiness. Indeed, there was something wary in the young man's eyes as he personally helped Danis down from her saddle. Gallarath was as handsome as ever, his movements smooth and firm as he stepped forward and bowed.

The First Daughter of Vanderthan dismounted and returned the king's bow before speaking. "I was sorry to hear about your father. Nevertheless, congratulations on your ascent to the throne. I know that you'll make Rochester a fine king."

"Why—thank you," replied Gallarath, still regarding the visitors nervously. "And to what do we owe the honor of this visit?" His eyes fixed upon Holt with an expression of almost desperate curiosity.

"Tellist informs us you have a seer of some repute. We are hoping that he might be able to give us some very important information," the princess explained.

"Oh? Oh! Why, of course!" The monarch turned to the short fellow at his side. "Whisktale, your reputation spreads even beyond my kingdom. You should be proud!"

"Oh, I *am,* Sire, most sincerely," declared the little man, bobbing his head up and down while those red, glittering eyes fastened upon Danis Vanderthan. He rubbed a hand across the thin, greasy hair plastered to his scalp, and then beamed with eagerness.

"Whisktale really *is* remarkable," Gallarath declared expansively. "Why, when he first arrived here—early in the winter, it was—he predicted the rat-plague you might have noticed in my city. And several days ago, he foresaw that you would be coming to visit. Now, come in—come in! We'll feast, and you can tell us what you need!"

The king seemed relaxed, now, as he offered the princess his arm. Quickly opening her saddlebag and retrieving the satchel containing the Crown of Vanderthan, Danis allowed him to escort them into the great, smoky hall that filled most of the lower level of Castle Rochester.

Holt chatted with Prince Wallas, who seemed older, more settled than when they had met the previous year. At that time the younger prince of Rochester had been an untested warrior. Wallas had enthusiastically accompanied his older brother as the army of Rochester allied with Vanderthan, turning aside an invasion. Now, as Wallas welcomed the Daryman and his companions with real sincerity, he seemed well content in his surroundings.

He was born a nobleman—he *should* be happy, Holt thought, with an undertone of resentment that startled him.

The seer, Whisktale, followed along as they made their way to seats at the great table that stood before the hall's huge fireplace. The snarling head of a blue-skinned bull leered at them from high on the wall. Holt remembered that Gallarath's full title included "Slayer of the Blue Gorgon," and he knew this horrific visage was the mortal remnant of that redoubtable foe.

"Did I tell you that I'll be married this summer?" Gallarath asked. "To a nice young lady, one of those who attends my mother's court."

"No, you didn't—but it seems that additional congratulations are in order," Danis replied, smiling.

Abruptly Holt had to suppress a laugh, as he remembered the king's earlier uneasiness. Gallarath had been afraid Danis had changed her mind, that she had decided to marry the King of Rochester, after all! The realization was amusing and, the Daryman had to admit, something of a relief. At the same time, he understood the decision—from Gallarath's point of view. During the course of their adventures, as the prince had won the contest for Danis's hand, Gallarath had realized what a strong-willed and determined woman the princess was. Though he had played the part of the jilted suitor—even, briefly, preparing to duel Holt—he had no doubt realized that Danis Vanderthan would never be the type of docile and compliant wife he desired.

"Now, tell me about this matter upon which you require Whisktale's help," the king suggested, after they had been served drinks, bread, and a passable—not Oxvale-quality—cheese.

Danis looked at the royal adviser, and Holt sensed her skepticism, though not a trace showed on her face. Admittedly, Whisktale did not look anything like the wise seer they had imagined. Beyond his beady, bloodshot eyes and pointed nose, the adviser to King Gallarath had virtually no chin. His head bobbed up and down eagerly between his rounded shoulders, as if he sniffed for some clue as to the companions' needs.

"Indeed, Sire—these are the heroes that I saw in the prophecy. They are embarked on an important quest, but I sense that they must gain crucial information before they continue. How may I be of service?"

Apparently deciding they had no better alternative, Danis Vanderthan placed the crown on the table before her and spoke. "We need to know how this can be destroyed."

For a time the seer didn't speak. Instead, he inspected the artifact visually, his eyes glittering like the rubies in the circlet's rim. "It will not be easy—but, if I am correct, there is a way," Whisktale declared, his voice husky. "Bring me my brazier!"

Servants soon produced a small iron pot, into which had been laid of bed of hot coals. The seer took several powders and a small vial from pockets in his voluminous robe. Bending over the coals, he began a mystical chant in a language unlike anything Holt had ever heard. When Whisktale dropped a pinch of powder into the brazier, a thin column of greenish, vaguely glowing mist arose, twisting and seething, into the air.

Immortal Game

The seer dropped bits of this and that into the coals, and slowly the smoke coalesced into a semi-solid cloud. It did not expand, but rather seemed to hold its shape and size, growing opaque as more and more smoke spewed upward. The red eyes flashed, locking on the crown, and then Whisktale turned toward the vaporous column again, studying symbols visible only to himself—at least, the Daryman didn't see anything other than the oddly colored smoke.

Holt saw Danis reach out, very slowly, to take the crown in her hands. With cool deliberation, she lifted it and placed it on her head.

Immediately her face became blank, aloof and uncaring. Holt had seen that expression on the princess, had even experienced the magical distancing himself the one time he had worn the platinum circlet. He couldn't suppress a shudder of unease, remembering the great power of the crown—it gave its wearer keen intuition and awesome protections. At the same time, it raised powerful barriers to emotions, effects that all but removed the wearer from the bounds of humanity. While she wore the crown, Danis might know much, but she would feel virtually nothing.

Now her green eyes, the shade of the ice on a deep, frozen lake, fastened unblinkingly on the seer.

Whisktale sprinkled a few drops of liquid from his vial onto the coals, and the gray smoke cloud abruptly became black. Flashes of color, tiny bolts of yellow and red lightning, crackled through the cloud. The seer's red eyes crossed as he fixed them upon those sparkles of brightness.

"Grant me the power to give the great princess her answer," chanted Whisktale. "Show me the knowledge that she seeks, so that I may share it!"

The lightning grew more frequent, until the cloud flickered from the violence of its internal storm. Abruptly Whisktale's voice fell, and his next words were growled thickly.

"Take the crown to the highest mountain of the Wyrmrange . . . there, amid the smoking heights, fires burn—fires of many kinds, hungry and consuming . . . there you will find that which you seek, the power to destroy the crown . . . there your quest will end. . . ."

Abruptly, gasping as if in pain, the seer toppled over backward, his back arched stiffly. The thick cloud broke from its magical boundary, dissipating through the hall like the smoke from a fireplace. Gagging and choking, Whisktale sat up, shaking his head.

"What–what happened?" he asked. "What did you learn?"

Danis slowly, deliberately removed the crown. The ice melted in her eyes, but the firm set of her chin was a clear sign of anger.

"I learned very much, Whisktale Seer," she declared grimly.

Instinctively Holt's hand tightened around his sword—he didn't breathe as he waited for her next words.

"I saw your true nature, your true soul!" she spat furiously. "And it was a heart, a soul of *Entropy!* You're a vile and spiteful creature, one who deceives Gallarath with evil—and who sought to deceive *me!*"

"Now see here—ulp!" Gallarath started to speak, then clapped shut his mouth at a fierce look from Danis.

Holt pushed back his chair, standing quickly, ready to draw his sword.

Whisktale too stood, sputtering indignantly. "Lies!" he cried. "It is you who—"

"I name you—*Rat!*" shrieked Danis, pointing an accusing finger. "You are corruption itself!"

The seer staggered backward, his eyes wild. He began to shrink, hunching over, crouching toward the floor. Wicked claws emerged from his sleeves and a naked, pale tail sprouted, lashing the stone floor behind him. Whiskers suddenly bristled beside that pointed nose, and abruptly the red eyes were shockingly familiar—the Daryman had seen the same crimson orbs on the rats that had thronged the streets of Rochester!

"Guards! Seize him!" shouted Gallarath, recovering from his own shock.

Bobbing back and forth on the floor, Whisktale opened his jaws and hissed. As Holt leapt the table

and men-at-arms surged inward from the doors, the giant rat turned and raced from the hall, dodging several guards who tried to chop him with their swords. With a flick of that ghastly tail, the hideous monster disappeared into the growing darkness beyond. Howls of rage and fear rang through the hall, marking the dwindling sounds of pursuit.

"The traitorous wretch!" growled Gallarath. "Who—or *what*—is he?"

"A wererat," Syssal Kipican observed. "Close cousin to the werewolf, though more craven—and prone to deceit. The crown enabled you to see his true form?"

"Yes—I saw his true form, but also something else."

"What?" pressed Holt.

She shook her head, reluctant to say anything. When she finally spoke, her words were hesitant.

"He told us of that place . . . the Wyrmrange. He said our quest would end there—that we would be able to destroy the crown! And when he said those words, I'm certain that he spoke the truth."

6
Paths to the Wyrmrange

"I don't really know where he came from. He arrived during the winter, around the time of my father's death, talking about fortunes and portents and the like. He used that brazier, looked into the smoke, and told me that Rochester was about to suffer a plague of rats." King Gallarath scratched his head and frowned at the memory.

"Of course—because he commanded the rats!" said Holt. "He *brought* them here!"

"True . . . though other things he's predicted have also come true. Two days ago he predicted I would have a royal visitor."

"That's exactly the time we left Tellist's lab," Danis observed.

"We know that the powers of Entropy are everywhere—it would have been easy for some creature of darkness to carry word to Rochester," Holt argued. "Spies watching the trail . . . someone who saw us ride out of Stone Bank and immediately sent word to Whisktale!"

"But about the Wyrmrange?" Gallarath asked of Danis. "You said you felt sure he was telling the truth?"

"Yes—at least so far as Whisktale believed, we will find the means to destroy the crown in the Wyrmrange."

"What is this range?" Holt inquired. "I've never heard of it before."

"Towering mountains, greater than the Trollheights, rising in the far reaches of Karawenn," Syssal Kipican explained. "Beyond even the realms of men and elves."

"I've heard that a distant clan of dwarves live in a place called the Dragon Mountains," Fenrald noted. "Could that be the same?"

"Possibly. I know that the Wyrmrange lies far beyond the borders of my kingdom," Gallarath said. "On one of my most epic hunting trips, I saw the tips of the mountains against the sky—and a rugged skyline it is, I assure you."

"Why is it called the Wyrmrange?" Fenrald

probed.

"Well, er—it's just conjecture, actually, goes back hundreds of years. It seems that, at one time, these mountains were the homes of Karawenn's dragons."

"Dragons? You mean fire-breathing, flying serpents?" asked Danis. "They don't really exist, do they?"

"Tut, tut—don't be too quick to discount something merely because you've never seen it," Tellist counseled.

"Aye—the lore of the elves tells of such creatures, though they were banished from the lowlands in ancient times," Syssal added. "Still, they must have gone somewhere. This Wyrmrange sounds like a pretty likely place."

"Well, if that's where the crown can be destroyed, that's where I'm going!" Danis declared with her customary decisiveness.

"I say—I think you're right that this is where the crown can be destroyed. But perhaps, my dear, you would consider allowing us to carry out this portion of the quest." With a gesture of his wings, Sir Ira swept Holt, Tellist Tizzit, Fenrald, and Syssal into his suggestion. "You could stay here and await our safe return."

Danis smiled as she shook her head. "That's a brave offer, my friend—and one that I'm sure you all would make willingly. But this crown is tied to my destiny, and I must go myself. I'm sincerely grateful I have loyal friends to accompany me."

Holt, too, would have pressed Sir Ira's arguments, but he had known the princess for too long to even attempt to change her mind. The companions stayed the night in the sumptuous guest quarters of Castle Rochester, on guard against rats and other threats. Nothing disturbed their slumber, but nevertheless, the solid walls, the soft warmth of beds and quilts, were little comfort in the light of the supernatural dangers they had encountered. In the morning, the companions awakened fully as stiff and restless as from any half-night's sleep on the hard ground.

The king and Wallas saw the small party off. The horses of the companions, at least, had benefitted from the stay—Gallarath's grooms had brushed them all thoroughly, repairing some loose horseshoes and combing manes until even Tellist's nag looked spritely.

"I'll take a company of men and ride to Vanderton," offered Prince Wallas. "We can make sure your father knows about Gazzrick."

"Thank you," Danis said, giving the young prince a hug.

"Farewell, Princess—and good luck," declared the king of Rochester. "I've seen that all your saddlebags are well laden with trail fare—I don't think you can count on foraging for food where you're going." He extended a formal hand, but Danis clasped Gallarath, too, in an embrace.

"Thanks for your help—and for the good wishes," she replied.

Sir Ira winged skyward while the five riders cantered along the muddy streets of Rochester. Holt noticed that the plague of rats, so numerous a day before, was nowhere in evidence. The party trotted through the city gates and started across the flat prairie beyond. The palisades of Castle Rochester swiftly dwindled in the distance, and within a few hours of their departure, the riders were crossing an apparently endless sea of grass.

For several days, they skirted the large realm of Darwill, passing through bleak country that was a far cry from the fertile farms and vales of Vanderthan. The scattered villages were really just collections of a few houses, perhaps with a blacksmith shop or a mill. Few offered even a ramshackle inn, but the companions remained content to sleep outside, maintaining watches through the moonless nights and starting on the trail each morning with the first sign of dawn.

As the days passed, they came to large stretches of forest, and the farmsteads became even fewer and more ragged. The moon re-emerged as a sliver visible in the morning sky, growing ever wider with each night. The travelers maintained their relentless watchfulness, but no threats of Entropy appeared to menace them.

One morning, the far horizon seemed to rise into a solid bank of clouds, but gradually the companions discerned a distant range of mountains. These summits rose stark against the sky, higher and more forbidding even than the Trollheights. A gray overcast lingered constantly over the heights, sometimes obscuring the summits and other times rising for a moment above the shadowy outlines of peak and ridgeline.

At the same time, the landscape grew more bleak, and the last of the human settlements fell behind. For more days they rode, seeing no sign of village nor farm. The stark forests bristled with brown, wasted pines. A wealth of dry needles covered the ground, and very little green showed at the tips of the brittle branches.

The terrain became rougher, rising into rocky heights that reminded Holt of the Knollbarrens, the rugged hunting grounds of his youth. Yet the valleys around them lacked the greenery, the pure and verdant vitality of the 'Barrens. The Daryman was glad Gallarath had been so generous with supplies, for game animals seemed to be nonexistent in this part of Karawenn.

Perhaps it was the lack of water. They crossed occasional shallow streams, but saw no lakes or ponds, and no indication of any waterway even a fraction the width of the mighty Tannyv. The very air smelled fetid, stinking of rotting vegetation.

The companions now took care to boil all their drinking water, for the sluggish creeks were murky and stagnant. After a week of warm, strong-tasting water, Holt began to have dreams about a cool and clear stream—while Fenrald complained that he'd give his pony, his weapon, and his bedroll to whoever could provide him with a cold pitcher of ale.

Gradually the mountains sorted themselves into individual peaks and specific, soaring ridges—still shaded by that eternal layer of clouds. The companions rode up steep trails, pushing through the foothills, leaving the brittle forests of the lowlands behind. Bleak as those woods had been, Holt found himself missing the trees as the company crossed through valleys lined with brown grass and flanked by looming shoulders of barren, craggy rock. The region was a wilderness of desolation.

The riders finally passed underneath the heavy overcast, and Holt felt as though they'd said goodbye to the sun—perhaps forever. The moon, which had grown to a half-circle during their journey, no longer lit their nights.

Then, in one of the higher valleys, the riders finally came across signs of life—at least, proof that someone else had been here at some unknown time in the past. Up on the slope of a steeply rising wall, Holt spotted a series of dark holes—cave mouths, apparently, but drilled in a precise row, all at the same elevation. Beneath each aperture spilled a fan of broken rock and rubble.

"Mines," Fenrald said with certainty. "And a

good high lot of ore there must have been, for someone to excavate on the side of a cliff like that!"

"Dwarven mines?" asked Holt.

"Hard to tell. They're obviously abandoned, whoever once dug them." He paused, and scratched his pate. "These don't look like ore-bearing mountains, but looks can fool you. Let's keep our eyes open—where there's this one excavation, there's bound to be more."

Over subsequent ridges, they found further evidence of digging as they followed a generally wide series of valleys toward the heights of the forbidding range. Finally, they encountered a mine shaft very near the foot of the slope, and Fenrald and Holt rode over to investigate while the other companions rested.

The shaft had a narrow, low entrance and was bored straight into the side of the hill. Fenrald stepped closer and ducked his head to peer inside.

"That cinches it—too low for dwarves. I think these valleys were once mined by gnomes. That explains about the mountains, too. No metal around here."

"What did the gnomes dig up, then?" asked the Daryman.

"Gems, I'll bet. That's what drives them little fellows crazy—sparkling stones of any color. Sure, they do find enough metal when they want, but show a gnome a diamond or a ruby and you'll see him drool right on the floor!"

Holt looked at the solid timbers shoring up the mine entrance, then kicked through the thin layer of dust lining the floor. "It seems sturdy enough, but I don't think anyone's used it recently."

"Nope. Maybe their stones played out, and they went somewhere else," Fenrald said tentatively, clearly unsure what caused the gnomes' disappearance. "But there's no sign of rot on the shoring timbers—I'd say this hasn't been abandoned for more than a few years, at most."

Again the travelers rode onward, and now they followed a kind of road—narrow, steep, and twisting, but smooth-surfaced and dry—that had been excavated into the climbing slopes. The width and pitch of that avenue, Fenrald pronounced, showed clearly its gnomish origin. Entrances to mines were visible in every valley they discovered, but nowhere was there any sign of active habitation. Instead, it seemed as though the black holes in the mountainsides had become haunted peepholes, where the ruins of a vanished people looked down on these interlopers, brave—or foolish—enough to travel here now.

Topping yet another in a succession of climbing ridges, Holt reined back in shock. "It's the gnomish city!" he guessed. "Or at least, it *was*."

Jagged shapes rose in the sheltered niche of a curving cliff. Shattered stones were scattered about in regular patterns, suggesting an ancient and long-abandoned ruin. As the riders drew closer, the Daryman sat silently in his saddle, wondering at the vast size of this onetime city.

Regular outlines of crumbled rock seemed to indicate that great edifices had once stood in this place, though now only the layout of their walls could be seen. Gusts of wind eddied in corners, stirring dry leaves—but little else—among the tangle of ruins that sprawled across the floor of this vale. Stone walls with ragged tops were the only remnants of many houses, some that indicated large rooms, and others suggesting mere cubicles. None of the buildings had roofs, and many of the walls had been smashed to the ground.

The companions rode through the wreckage in silence. Despite the rubble strewn everywhere, the layout of the streets was still visible. Holt gradually decided that his earlier impression—that this was an ancient ruin—was wrong. He saw splinters of dry wood and charcoal in some of the shattered buildings, even places where cloth and woolen material, sodden and dirty, still lay among the broken stones. This city had been reduced to ruin, certainly, but the wrack had not been centuries, nor even decades ago.

Still, there was no sign of life here now. Instead, sooty outlines darkened many walls, small figures silhouetted in black char. Danis shuddered visibly at the sight of these, and Sir Ira touched her shoulder with a brown-feathered wing. Holt tried to avoid thinking of the scalding horror that must have ravaged this place. The remains of beams and other woodwork was all charred, and the loose refuse on the floors seemed as if it might once have been ashes.

Tellist, white-faced, reined in Dragonfire and held his head downcast, unwilling any longer to look at the devastation. Huge stones lay scattered chaotically, square blocks shattered by unimaginable force. A mournful wind moaned through the ruins, swirling mini-tornadoes of dust between the broken structures. The air was harsh and dry, smelling of parched ground and ashes, with a barren taint as lifeless as any desert zephyr.

"Look at this," Fenrald called somberly, and the others gathered around. The dwarf gestured toward the remains of a stout metal door. Something with crushing force had wrenched it from its hinges, twisting it violently. Several deep gouges, the scrapes of incredibly powerful claws, marred the hard metal surface.

They looked upward then at the mountains that towered all around. Each of them remembered the tales of fire-breathing serpents, stories that had seemed, from the safety of a stone-walled castle, laughable yarns out of a fairy tale. Now they saw the ruins of this gnomish city, and the mighty, barren peaks that loomed beyond.

And tales of dragons were not hard to believe.

7
The Shattered Wall

An air of death, of desolation and abandonment, clung to the ruins like a sodden cloak, oppressing the companions with its gloomy weight. Though the hour was late, they forged on without discussion—each wanted to get as far as possible from the doomed village before sunset.

The roadway rose into the mountains beyond, narrowing and growing steeper. Holt and Syssal took turns leading, at times dismounting to guide the horses on foot up the grade. For the most part, the companions were restricted to single file on the steep track, while Sir Ira soared ahead, scouring the trail for threats and seeking possible alternate routes.

The horses, even Dragonfire, did well enough along this stretch. Holt noticed that Tellist Tizzit, however, was frequently straining for breath. The Daryman suggested many halts, yet even after a few minutes of rest the ancient wizard remained red-faced and wheezing.

The roadway switched back and forth along the face of a nearly vertical bluff. For an hour, Holt's lungs burned, forcing him to pause, gasping for breath, every few minutes. Finally, the grade eased, and he led the companions into another mountain valley, relieved to discover a section of level ground.

The valley floor curved between two great mountains, but beyond those summits a third massif rose into the sky. Faces of dark slate, gray and forbidding, slick and black where water trickled over the stone, rose into massive, splintered ridges. Broken overhangs of jagged stone quashed any thought of a climb, and even the saddles between the peaks surmounted a thousand feet or more of sheer, barren cliff. The trail twisted around the foot of a steep slope, then abruptly vanished into the tangle of a rockslide. Rocky cliffs rose to all three directions beyond the pile of boulders.

"The road must have led somewhere," Syssal said somberly, echoing Holt's unspoken apprehensions. The companions skirted the rockslide, following the valley floor toward the greatest of the three mountains. Slopes rose to all sides, impassable barriers.

Beside them splashed a shallow stream with traces of steam wisping from the surface, bringing the bitter taint of sulphur to Holt's nostrils. The Daryman reached down to touch the clear water and was startled to find that it was warm, almost uncomfortably hot. He shuddered. These mountains were increasingly unnatural and bizarre.

"There's hot springs under the ground," Fenrald explained when the Daryman remarked on his discovery. "Not too many of 'em around Graywall, but they're not unheard of. From the way these mountains are steaming and smoking, I'd say this underground heat is a lot more common here in the Wyrmrange."

Holt wondered at the power embodied in these mountains—capable of burning rocks, of heating streams and sending clouds of smoke and ash billowing upward to obscure the sky. The valley floor, shrouded in the shadows of that eternal overcast, continued toward the great mountain. Only at the last minute did it veer to skirt the boulder-strewn foot of the rocky giant.

Sir Ira soared around the massif and returned to settle onto his customary perch on Lancer's saddle. "Sad to say, there doesn't seem to be anywhere to go from here. The valley reaches the cliff between these three peaks, and it just stops."

In a few minutes, the riders drew up at the base
of a rock-walled precipice. There was no sign of a
mine, or any other kind of passageway.

"Doesn't make sense to me!" Fenrald declared,
stalking forward and knocking at several of the
rocks with his hammer. Loose stones tumbled and
clattered downward. "That road came into this
valley, and the gnomes put a lot of work into
bringing it here. But there's no mines, no houses—
nothing! Why?"

Holt picked at the rock with his knife blade,
and he, too, found the stone to be firm and hard.
Danis turned around and unhooked the strap of
her saddlebag. Only as the Daryman saw the silver circlet in her hands did he understand her
idea.

"Wait!" he cried.

"The crown may allow me to see more than we
can right now," the princess replied firmly. "I don't
see that we have any choice—other than to turn
back!"

Biting back his objections, knowing he wouldn't
be able to change her mind, Holt watched tensely.
Danis set the crown on her head, and her face
went blank. She stared at the wall of stone, then
nodded.

"Strike the cliff with your sword."

She spoke the command to Holt, and he turned
toward the wall, drawing the weapon before he
even realized what he was doing. With an effort

he stopped, twisting back to face her.

"I touched it," he said. "It's solid—it might break the—"

"Do it!" she snapped, her words strong enough to spin him around. He stumbled toward the cliff, trying to ignore the pain in his heart. At the same time, he couldn't ignore the force of her command, so compellingly did the artifact's power burn his will. It's the crown, he reminded himself—though the knowledge was bitter consolation.

He raised the Lodestone Blade, taking the hilt in both hands. His body coiled springlike before he smashed the weapon hard against the dark granite. Stone shattered, and he immediately feared the ancient weapon had broken. Then Fenrald grabbed his shoulder, pulling him several steps backward, and the Daryman realized his blade was as solid as ever.

Gaping upward in mute astonishment, he watched as shards of the cliff tumbled outward, breaking from the mountain face with crackling force. But the stone did not fall in huge slabs of rock—instead, it was more like a shower of glass, as if a hard, nearly impervious surface had shattered, and now the slivers tumbled into the dust before the astonished travelers.

Crashes rang and echoed through the mountain vale, tinkling musically as the shards struck ground and broke into smaller pieces. Glittering like diamonds, dust billowed upward. Then even the shards disappeared, as the pieces dissolved into a fine powder, churning and expanding like smoke.

The dwarf and the Daryman scrambled farther back as the cloud rose from the wreckage. Looking over the debris, Holt saw that a narrow gap had been revealed—a cut in the rock that created a gorge between these two massive summits. The gnomish road followed the floor of this deep passage, twisting forward to quickly vanish around a bend in the shadowy corridor.

"Tut, tut—some kind of magical barrier, I should say," Tellist Tizzit observed. "Of course, a little more solid than the usual—but no match for trained magical inspection!"

"Proceed—at once!" commanded the princess.

Holt took a step forward, then determinedly forced himself to halt. "No!" he declared, looking into those piercing, ice-shrouded eyes. "Not until you take the crown off."

Danis opened her mouth to speak. She could command him, and if she exerted her will, Holt could not resist. But he met her cold gaze with a fierce look of his own, desperately hoping his presence, his emotion, might somehow seep through the veil raised by the Crown of Vanderthan.

Abruptly, the princess closed her mouth. She sat in Lancer's saddle, lost in thought. Holt had the feeling her companions might have been a hundred miles away, for all the notice she took of them. Slowly, with visible reluctance, she reached upward, touching the crown but not lifting it from her head.

Then, in a smooth gesture, she whisked it off and held it against her body, as if fearing someone would try to snatch it away. Danis looked around wildly, all but gasping for breath. Her eyes met Holt's, and he saw the pain there.

"It—it was hard to take it off," she said. "Harder than ever before—it *frightened* me!"

"Best to keep that thing wrapped up tight from now on," Fenrald said bluntly, echoing Holt's feelings exactly. "Let's have a look at the rest of this road."

Somberly, Holt moved into the narrow passageway, leading Old Thunder by the reins. Danis came behind with Lancer and Sir Ira, while Syssal, Tellist, and Fenrald completed the single file.

The stone walls soared to either side, so precipitous that sometimes they seemed to merge into a lofty roof. Even in places where he could look up and see the sky, Holt observed only a narrow crack, a gap between the cliffs that allowed merely a glimpse of smoky, leaden overcast. The shadows in the floor of the gorge were as thick as a cloudy night.

Despite the altitude and the lack of sunlight, the gorge proved surprisingly warm. The stone walls radiated heat like any sun-soaked boulders, and the air was thick and humid, more like the miasma of a swamp than the breezy coolness of a high mountain vale.

Another thought occurred to Holt as he followed the endless series of twists and turns. Sunset was near, and once night fell, the shadows in this narrow gorge would be absolute. He picked up his pace, hoping to reach an end to the notch before dark. Someone—the gnomes, presumably—had smoothed off any protuberances on the walls, so that the cliffs never closed any tighter than the bed of the roadway. In places, both walls rose straight up from the edges of the track, but even here they could pass without scraping against the cliffs.

Abruptly Holt saw a brightening in the pathway before them, an illumination beyond the next few bends. The light increased in strength, and when he came around the last turn he had to shade his eyes against the brilliant setting sun.

He stepped out of the gorge onto ground covered by soft grass, the fringe of a wide, bowl-shaped valley. The sun approached the opposite rim of the vale, low enough that the slanting rays lit the bottom of the churning overcast. For once, the oppressive clouds actually looked beautiful, passing through shades of red, orange, and purple.

A cool, refreshing breeze washed across Holt, soothing away the sweat and heat of the passage through the rocks. As the others emerged to join him on the grassy hillside, they raised their faces into the wind, letting the sunlight and dry air soothe them.

"It's beautiful," Danis said, summing up all their thoughts as she looked below.

Indeed, as Holt's eyes adjusted to the brightness and he began to look around this huge, sheltered vale, he was stunned by the pastoral allure of this place. Though ringed all around by lofty, unclimbable cliffs, the valley itself might have been some lowland hamlet, thriving in a climate of plentiful rainfall and warm temperatures. Even the sky was different, as the clouds themselves seemed to be held at bay by the boundaries of this secluded vale.

Waterfalls spumed down the cliffs in several locations, and large lakes and placid ponds dotted the valley floor, reflecting the brilliant cloud-colors of the sunset. Lush groves of broad-leaved trees thrived throughout the place, though these were often broken by meadows and other clearings—some with a smooth, green uniformity that looked very much like pastureland.

"Look—smoke!" Danis declared, indicating a plume of vapor wafting through the air to one side.

"There's a building," Holt confirmed.

A small mill stood beside one of the nearer ponds, and several stone bridges arched across streams here and there throughout the valley. Around one of the lakes, lights gradually twinkled into view, as if lamps had been lit in the windows of countless small houses.

"It's like a—a hidden wonderland," the princess declared, waving her hand over the fields and forests.

"Who would have thought a place like this could survive in these barren mountains?" Holt wondered aloud. Parts of the pastoral scene reminded him of Oxvale, though this place seemed even more peaceful than his quaint and quiet village.

"Let's go down the hill," Fenrald suggested. "At least we can find a place to camp in those woods. We can look around a little bit, get our bearings, in the morning."

"Splendid idea," Sir Ira said. He took to the air and glided ahead, returning a few minutes later to report that the forest floor was smooth and open, with plenty of grass and clover for the horses.

Holt looked backward to see that the gorge of the gnomish road entered this valley through the side of what was otherwise an unbroken ring of cliffs. Remembering the destruction they had earlier encountered, and the magical screen that had guarded this vale, the Daryman realized that the inhabitants might have good reason to keep intruders at bay. The place was so pastoral and serene, however, that he couldn't believe its residents could turn out to be enemies.

The weary travelers entered the cool stillness of the forest and made camp beside a narrow brook. Trout flitted through the clear water, but the companions decided to eat from their provisions, since night was falling.

As they settled down, Holt suddenly felt a tickling on the back of his neck. Instinctively he brushed his hand across his skin, swiping at an imaginary insect—and realizing at the same time that he was not reacting to any physical touch. He shuddered with the distinct feeling that something was watching him. Whirling around, the Daryman confronted only the heavy, gnarled trunks of ancient oaks. Just spooked, he decided—after all, they had been on guard for very many days now.

"What was that?" demanded Fenrald, abruptly rising and scowling at the woods. Holt felt certain then that he hadn't imagined the presence—after all, it wasn't like the pragmatic dwarf to get spooked by wind or squirrels. His hand resting on the hilt of his sword, the Daryman heard tiny sounds of rustling, saw shadowy images of movement in the darkness.

"It would appear that we're surrounded," Syssal Kipican said quietly. The Daryman remembered that the elf's eyes were exceptionally keen, especially at night—but it galled him that he, himself, could see nothing of any threat.

"Who's there?" Danis demanded. "Show yourself! We come in peace, and mean you no harm."

In reply they heard a scurrying and rustling in the leaves. The elf was right—the noises came from all around them.

Then, hesitantly, several figures advanced from the ring of darkness. Though he couldn't make out details at first, the Daryman saw that the strangers were folk of several different sizes and postures. One of them seemed to be mounted, but when the rider spoke, Holt realized the man-like head and face was actually a *part* of the steed—a human's torso atop the shoulders of a large horse!

"Who are you to knock down the barrier of Rift-vale?" demanded the hulking creature. He strutted out of the darkness, gesturing with a large lance.

"We ought to kill you now!" growled another. This fellow hobbled awkwardly forward. His facial features and speech were human, but his legs were cloaked in fur, and terminated in cloven, goatlike hooves.

"They're the first through the crystal wall—but you can bet there'll be others soon behind!" Another figure, shorter than Fenrald but bearded like a dwarf, spoke. Holt saw that the creature bore a stout, heavy crossbow. The steel arrowhead glinted in the starlight, aimed carefully at the princess.

"Wait!" the Daryman protested. "We're not here

to harm you! And there's no one else coming after—"

"Silence!" shouted the horse-man, brandishing his lance. "You are intruders—and destroyers of our protection, as well. As such, your fate has been decided. The only discussion from this point on shall determine the manner of your deaths!"

8
Riftvale

"What kind of people are you?" Holt demanded indignantly. "Why do you take us prisoner when we've done nothing to hurt you!"

"Silence! Spies and saboteurs, you are—no doubt yer but the vanguard of an army of wizards!" The gnomish fellow with the crossbow took a menacing step forward, squinting from above the great lump of his nose. His beard quivered in righteous indignation.

"They probably come from the dragon," hissed the goat-footed one, hopping up and down in agitation. "I say we sticks 'em right 'ere and be done with it!" The goat-man carried a stout staff, and he shook it toward the companions. "C'mon Gallut!" he said, addressing the hoofed lancer. "Stick 'em right now!"

"Don't try it!" Holt warned, resting his hand on the hilt of the Lodestone Blade. Now that he had a closer look at their assailants, he thought that perhaps the companions could fight their way out of the trap. Still, he didn't think the time was yet right to draw his sword.

His caution was rewarded as more bushes rustled. A number of stunted figures, all bearing the sturdy-looking crossbows, emerged from concealment to encircle the companions. Any attempt at violence would be met with a dozen sharp barbs— fired at point-blank range. With an effort of will, Holt forced his hands to fall loosely to his sides.

"You don't *look* like an army of wizards," squeaked a voice from an unseen source.

"We're *not—!*"

Holt paused, startled, as a small, girlish figure fluttered forward, tiny wings buzzing softly to hold her aloft. She hovered behind the front crossbowman. "Perhaps we should take them to the tarn and let the others help us decide."

"Fires at the tarn," snorted the goat-man. "Fires kin make these spies tell the truth!"

"Now, Snivyar," protested the fairy. "We have no call to be talking like that."

"I'm sure you don't," Fenrald Falwhak agreed,

making an effort to sound friendly. He addressed the little fellow. "You're a gnome, I see—well, we're practically cousins. I've got no doings with your enemies, you can be sure."

"I never had no cousins so big and so ugly," the gnome snapped. "Nor with such a tiny nose!"

"Yeah? Well, I wondered what that big knob on *your* face was for. Did you steal it off a moose?"

"Look!" Holt interjected forcefully. "We're not your cousins, but we're not your enemies, either! If you are kin to the gnomish folk who once lived beyond this valley, we know of your enemies—and we share them!"

"You are enemies of the dragon?" asked the fairy, buzzing around the gnome to listen.

"Then why did you break the Crystal Ward?" asked Gallut, the centaur. "That was our greatest barrier to the serpent!"

"We—we didn't know," Holt said.

"Tut, tut—I thought dragons could fly," noted Tellist. "How could such a wall protect you against the sky?"

"Magic!" retorted the short bowman. "It used to guard all of Riftvale, even the air—but now you've gone and smashed it!"

"Why did you destroy it?" demanded the centaur ominously.

"We tried to follow the road into the mountains," the Daryman explained patiently. "We wanted to proceed higher into the Wyrmrange—and this seemed the best way!"

"It is!" the fairy replied brightly. "The other side of our valley leads right—*ulp!*" She squeaked into silence as the centaur elbowed her roughly aside.

"But the ward was a powerful enchantment!" objected the gnome. "Rassletune himself said it would take an army of wizards to bash it down—and *you* bashed it down!"

"Not an army of wizards, but a sword," Holt said. He drew the weapon, displaying the blade of dull gray rock. "This is the Lodestone Blade, and it bears a power rooted in Karawenn itself. I struck the ward, and it collapsed around us."

"How do we know you don't make way for an army of wizards?" demanded the goatlike fellow who had been called Snivyar.

"Go and look!" Danis snapped.

"But how did you even know the Crystal Ward was there?" asked the fairy. "Didn't it look just like the mountain?"

"I saw it," the princess declared.

"When she saw the road ending before the rock," Holt said. "She guessed it had to continue on from there."

"I think we have to take them to the village," the gnome said.

"You're right, Gibblesnart," the centaur agreed. He still held the lance upraised. "But make any move that I don't like, and . . ." He snapped the weapon through the air to punctuate his threat, wielding the heavy lance like a human might brandish a sword.

Danis snatched the bundle of her bedroll from Lancer's saddlebags, lashing the cloak to her belt under the watchful eyes of their captors.

The companions were prodded along a woodland trail, forced to leave their horses behind—Snivyar promised, grudgingly, that they would be fed and cared for.

"We don't make war on dumb animals!" the gnome Gibblesnart declared.

Holt and Fenrald insisted that the companions be allowed to keep their weapons, and their captors apparently decided it was easier not to argue. Those gnomish arrows remained steady, poised to unleash a volley at a moment's notice.

As the procession marched along, more of the valley's inhabitants emerged from the brush, forming a growing procession. When they passed from the forest into a field of lush grass and flowers, the starlight allowed the companions to get a better look at their surroundings—and at the heavily armed members of their impromptu escort.

Two files of gnomes with crossbows flanked the prisoners, and the deadly weapons never wavered. Several centaurs pranced in the forefront, while a number of the goat-footed creatures scampered at the flanks and rear. The fairy, who alone among their captors seemed to be unarmed, hovered through the air near Gibblesnart, the gnome who appeared to be in command.

They came to the shore of a placid stream, and the lights of the village twinkled nearby. Holt squinted, certain he saw large, luminous eyes glowing at him from the waters. Slick-skinned creatures slipped along the bank, then vanished into the stream when the human stopped and stared. Prodding, the gnomes led them past a stone bridge, then crossed at a ford some distance farther down the brook. The companions soaked their boots and trousers to their knees, but each of the gnomes emerged shivering and sodden all the way to his chin. Only the crossbows, held high overhead, stayed dry.

"Why didn't we use the bridge?" Fenrald asked, perplexed and irritated.

"It's b—broken!" Gibblesnart explained. "Now m—move! Over to those fires!"

"What kind of runts are these—can't fix their own bridge!" Fenrald whispered scornfully to Holt.

That question wouldn't be answered during the night. The companions were led to a small hut and pushed inside, one after the other. Immediately the stout door slammed, and they heard a bar lower into place. The interior was illuminated only by a small high window, too small for even Syssal to wriggle through. The walls were bare, and the hut was furnished with only a few rough benches and straw mats resting on the dirt floor.

Shortly afterward, hoarse voices and lusty arguments reached their ears. By standing on one of the benches, Holt was able to stretch upward and look out the high window at the village.

"What is it? What's going on?" asked Fenrald impatiently.

"I see a lot of people—centaurs, gnomes, fairies. There's dogs too. Everyone's gathered around a huge bonfire. Wow!"

"What? What do you see?" Danis demanded.

"A *tree!* It's marching up to the fire, crossing its branches—um, its arms—across its chest. I see kind of a face, outlined in knotholes. Looks like it's frowning."

"A treant," Syssal suggested thoughtfully. "Rare and magical creatures—but well in keeping for this company."

Pipe music trilled, incongruously, above the sounds of heated debate.

"Some of those goat-footed things are playing music and dancing!" the Daryman observed. "Everybody else is just arguing, but no one seems to be listening to anyone else. The tree-man is still standing there scowling at everybody."

"Satyrs—those are the 'goat-footed' things," Syssal explained. "And our horselike friend is a centaur. Rare folk, and, like the treant, quite magical."

"Not to mention the fairy and the gnomes," agreed Fenrald. "Altogether an odd lot—especially to be sharing the same village!"

"And what about the water?" remembered the

Daryman. "I'm sure I saw some creatures down in the streambed, near that bridge."

"Nixies, most likely," guessed the elf. "Like fairies—but of course they live in streams and ponds. Another unique and magical resident of this secret valley."

"Quite so. Nixies, I mean—and a bit worried they are, too. Everyone who lives here, to tell the truth," Tellist Tizzit declared. "Even if I'm not an army of wizards, I did a little exploring. I know that all these folk—of Riftvale, they call it—are terribly frightened."

"How can you know that?" Danis wondered.

"A simple spell of mind reading—no trouble at all. I just listened to their thoughts while we were walking to the village."

"What are they worried about?" asked Holt skeptically.

"It seems they've lost their king. Things are just not the same without him. There're berries rotting on bushes, milk spoiling in the barns, without the work being done."

"How did they lose the king?"

"He died—as to how, I don't know. Nobody thought about that while I was paying attention."

"That's why there's all this bickering," Holt guessed. "Nobody wants to give in to anyone else."

"That's right," Tellist agreed. "When we passed that bridge, both the gnomes and the centaurs were grousing to themselves about it—and about

114

how the other fellows were too stubborn to fix it!"

"What's going on now?" asked Fenrald, as the music outside rose to a higher pitch. The voices of argument had merged, until all the sounds pulsed like a chant.

Holt looked out the window. "Now they're *all* dancing. Those satyrs are swinging fairies around. Even the centaurs are kicking up their heels."

"Typical," groused Fenrald. "These are flighty folk, even the gnomes," he admitted. "Not stable, hard-working, solid people like dwarves."

"These fairy-folk seem to have a little more fun than some dwarves I've known," Syssal said with a rueful laugh. "Not that it gets us any closer to getting out of here."

"I don't think we'd have trouble getting out of here," Danis said, pushing at the door. Though solid, it wobbled slightly, and Holt suspected they could force it open with a good shove. "Still, I don't know if escape is the best thing we can do."

"What do you mean?" Fenrald asked indignantly. "I think we should put some space between ourselves and this village—as soon as these guys go to sleep!"

"Where would we go?" asked the princess. "Back down from the mountains?"

"No," Holt chimed in. "I think our best path goes right through Riftvale. We just have to get them to show us where it is."

"And to let us follow it," Syssal noted. "But yes, I

think you've got the right idea."

The Daryman continued to observe the village. "Now they're arguing again—something about going to bed hungry. The gnomes are stomping off, and I don't think the satyrs feel like playing anymore. They're just sitting there, moping. Except for the treant—it went back to the woods."

"Tut, tut—at least I haven't heard more talk about putting us to death. I don't mind telling you that business was getting me a little nervous," admitted the wizard.

"Can they really be flighty enough to forget something like that?" asked Holt.

"Who knows? The fairy-folk are capricious, even a trifle scatterbrained," Sir Ira hooted softly. "Perhaps they'll forget about us entirely by morning."

"Still, I don't see where this gets us. How do we get any favors from these lunatics?" demanded the dwarf.

"We help them," Sir Ira said. "It's simple, actually—we just give them the same kind of guidance a king would. I think that's all they need."

"What?" spluttered Fenrald.

"Well, something like this . . . ." The companions gathered together to hear Sir Ira's plan, and as the old bird outlined his idea, they all saw its potential. Holt and Danis added suggestions, until everyone had a part to play on the morrow. Finally, they slept.

It was several hours after dawn that they first

heard movement in the village—the clinking of dishpans, wells pumping, children scampering around in play. When they judged that most of the fairy-folk were up, Holt and Fenrald started shouting, calling for someone to let them out so they could walk around.

Shortly the door opened, and Gibblesnart peered in at them. The gnome wore a pair of battered trousers and blinked sleepily. "Walk around? It's not even noon yet!" he declared irritably.

"We like to start early," Holt explained, stepping past the yawning gnome and blinking in the bright sunlight. He moved casually, with elaborate unconcern, hoping that the little fellow was not inclined to remember the death sentence Gallut had pronounced the day before. Fortunately, Gibblesnart simply yawned and blinked, glaring around irritably but making no move to obstruct the prisoners.

Holt, Tellist, and Fenrald went immediately to the bridge beside the village. They saw that several of the stones had fallen into the stream, and that the structure did in fact crumble dangerously.

"It's not hopeless," Fenrald declared. "Just some shifted keystones."

Danis and Syssal, meanwhile, sat on several stumps and chatted with the fairy-folk children who were bold enough to approach. Soon they were surrounded by a throng of young gnomes, satyrs, and centaur colts, all jostling and pushing to get closer.

The elf demonstrated his ring of disguise, shifting his appearance from an old human woodsman to a handsome elven prince, from a sinister witch to a belligerent dwarf—one who bore a startling resemblance to Fenrald Falwhak.

"Who among you is the best at finding berries?" Danis asked, to a chorus of boastful replies.

"Say—I caught the delightful scent of fresh scallions in the woods," Sir Ira observed, with a palpably hungry sigh.

"Each of you who brings an armload of scallions will have a chance to choose a disguise for me!" Syssal declared, with an expansive wave of his hand. Dozens of squealing youngsters raced for the woods, eager to claim the prize.

Beside the sagging bridge, Fenrald waded into the stream. He and Holt began to pry at one keystone—a rock far too heavy for them to move by themselves. For several minutes they strained, conscious of a few gnomes and centaurs gathering around. The two friends ignored the observers, sweating and grunting from the efforts of their work.

"Here now, what's the point in that?" demanded Gallut, who shouldered his way through the centaurs. He held a coil of stout rope, and threw one end of the line to Holt. "Let's give it a little pull."

"Tsk. You'll need to pry it loose!" Gibblesnart argued. "Take that pole over there and—oh, by the

Spheres, let *me* do it!" Brooking no assistance, the gnome entered the stream and pried, while the centaurs hauled on the rope. Slowly the rock came free, until it was half out of the water.

"There—hold it just so!" Tellist declared. He muttered some words, scowled and scratched his head for a minute, then brightened. "Oh, yes!" He snapped his fingers and pointed, and the rock floated into the air.

The astonished Gibblesnart almost dropped his staff, while the centaurs gaped in amazement. Finally the gnome remembered his hands, reaching up to prod the floating stone into place with the tip of the pole.

"Get some mortar!" shouted a couple of satyrs, and several gnomes stepped forward with a tray full of pasty mix. They slopped the stuff around the stone, firmly sealing it into place.

"We'll have to lift the others," the wizard said apologetically. "My spell's only good for one. Still, that was the biggest."

As gnomes and centaurs bustled into the stream, hauling rocks and bracing the center of the stone span, Holt looked across the village. The young fairy-folk encircling Danis had scattered, but mounds of scallions were already gathered. The village's children had already raced off on the next part of the game. Holt's heart leapt at the sight of several young gnomes, arms laden, staggering into the village under heavy burdens. Hoot-

ing encouragements, Sir Ira praised each addition to the pile. Lurching to Danis and Syssal, they dumped dozens of ears of corn onto the ground.

"That's splendid!" Danis cried. "Ten ears, twelve—fourteen makes you the winner. But look—here come some more!"

Young centaurs arrived dragging sacks full of potatoes, while fairies fluttered in with their aprons filled with ripe berries of all colors. The contest progressed to mushrooms, rice, and nuts, all of which had ripened in Riftvale. Each gatherer vied to break the record, to bring back more than his fellows. As the game continued, the elder fairy-folk emerged, first to watch, and then to join in the gathering.

By sunset, the bridge was solidly patched, and the center of the village was filled with mounds of various foods, piled over the rim of every tub and bin that the fairy-folk owned. Cheers and music rang through the village, and Holt and his companions, weary but content, trudged toward the central circle.

Gibblesnart came over to the Daryman, the gnome's head bobbing up and down in pleasure. "You showed us pretty good," the little villager admitted as the companions joined in a great feast. "Me and Gallut've been talking. We think most of you can go, whenever you want."

"*Most* of us?" asked Holt, suddenly worried.

"Yup—most of you. Just one'll stay behind."

"What? Who?"

"One of you gots to stay here forever—to be our new king. You guys are all pretty smart. You pick the one to be king. Now, come on—Snivyar's ready to start the music."

Holt, stunned and dismayed, watched the jolly gnome clump away. The Daryman didn't really feel like dancing.

9
King of the Fairy-Folk

The gnomes showed no interest in further conversation. With bouncing enthusiasm, cheerful
laughter, and good-natured joking directed at their
centaur neighbors, they made preparations for a
major feast. The satyrs and fairies shared in the
exhilaration. Impromptu songs were raised, and
Snivyar led a parade of dancing, prancing villagers
around the huts and along the stream

The treant returned, marching slowly out of the
woods. Several saplings came hesitantly behind,
clustering around the shelter of the burly trunk.

Though the gnarl-faced creature remained somber, the broad and leafy branches were spread wide above the gathering—no longer did the tree-man cross his mighty limbs in suspicious aloofness.

Dogs barked around the procession, and Holt stared in astonishment as several of the agitated hounds vanished from sight, only to reappear in drooling, floppy-eared excitement on the other side of the parade.

Noting his amazement, Fenrald chuckled. "Blink dogs, they're called. Good hunters, and pretty rare, too."

Holt and Fenrald tromped to the nearby grove where the centaurs had taken their horses. They found that Old Thunder and the other steeds had not only been well fed, but rubbed and brushed as well. The big draft horse nickered appreciatively as Holton clapped him on the shoulder, then lowered his muzzle, returning his attentions to the lush clover that layered the ground in thick greenery.

"What are we going to do?" groaned the Daryman after checking to insure that none of the villagers were within earshot.

"We could try to escape when they're in the middle of their party," the dwarf suggested, without much hope.

"Escape to where? Back down to the plains? That's the same problem we had yesterday. No— we need them to show us the way to get higher into the mountains." Holt shook his head in despair. A voice in his mind suggested that he offer to stay behind, king-hostage to the fairy folk so that his companions could continue. Yet he knew he could never do this. Not only would he make a terrible king, but he felt certain Danis would need him—or at least, would need his sword—before this quest reached a conclusion.

Without arriving at any solution, the dwarf and the Daryman walked back to the village to Sir Ira and Danis. Tellist Tizzit had joined the dancing, though after a few spins with a squealing fairy, the wizard tottered back to his friends. Holt saw Syssal Kipican whirling through the frenzy, apparently enjoying himself, but the decision lurking over their heads laid a cloud even on the elf's golden face. Finally he, too, grew tired, and retreated to sit on the log beside Danis.

In the village center, satyrs piped, centaurs chanted, and all the folk of Riftvale skipped, hopped, and kicked up their heels—or hooves. Holt was amazed at their endurance, and at the beaming expressions of joy on the faces of centaurs, satyrs, gnomes, and sprites alike.

"They really *need* a king," Danis observed. "Look what we've done to their mood."

"There's none of that fighting we saw last night," Syssal agreed. "It's as if they've set aside all the grievances that had grown so deep between them."

"But we *can't* leave one of us behind!" the princess declared. "That's more like accepting a lifetime of captivity than ascending to a throne!"

"Perhaps you're right . . . but perhaps not," Sir Ira declared, clearing his throat theatrically.

"What do you mean?" Holt asked. "You can't think that we should just give in to them!"

"Well, as to that—I'm not sure we have a terribly great amount of choice in the matter. But there's another thing as well."

The others waited while the owl blinked his great yellow eyes, deep in thought. "As you know, I was lord of a small vale myself—in the Knollbarrens. It was an enchanted place, full of beauty and tranquility, until the coming of the nightshade."

Holt felt Danis shiver beside him, and he, too, felt an involuntary chill at the memory of that horrific beast. It had swept from the sky in killing frenzy, massive and black, destroying much Sir Ira's beautiful domain. The brutally powerful monster had nearly slain them all. Only the shelter of an underground burrow—and Holt's reckless courage in rescuing the princess—had enabled them to survive.

"Truth is," Sir Ira continued, "I really *miss* that place. Vanderthan is lovely, of course, and I can go anywhere in Karawenn that I want, but I have a sense of loss I've never been able to shake."

"Are you saying . . . Riftvale . . . you'd stay?" Danis asked slowly.

"I—I'm saying that these folk need somebody like me, and that—perhaps—I need somebodies like them.

"The truth is, when I made that suggestion about repairing the bridge, about making a game of gathering the food, that was the most useful I've felt in a long time. No, it's not giving up—it's rather like finding two pieces of a whole and fitting them nicely together."

The Daryman was about to argue further when he felt Danis's hand upon his arm, restraining him with gentle pressure. He looked at the princess, saw pain in her eyes, but also an understanding of Sir Ira's choice. She wanted Holt to understand as well.

And, just maybe, he did. He knew he would miss the owl terribly, but Sir Ira Hsiao would make a splendid king for these dwellers of Riftvale.

The others, too, sensed the rightness of the choice. It was Danis who rose and strode to the center of the celebration, while Sir Ira glided from his perch to light on her shoulder. Slowly the frenzy of dancing settled, and she was surrounded by a ring of bright-eyed, joyous villagers.

"Folk of Riftvale," she announced, her voice settling the last of the celebration into silence. "I bring to you one of great wisdom and kindness. It was he who fashioned the ideas that led to the repairing of your bridge—he who devised the game whereby you all gathered such a plentiful supply of food. He is a creature of fairy, and was once a ruler of his own realm.

"That realm is no more, but he has arrived at a new home—and a new throne. Fairy-folk of Rift-vale, I give you your new ruler: Sir—ah, *King* Ira Hsiao!"

The owl spread his wings to their broad span, nearly equal to the reach of Holt's arms. He raised himself to his full height, and dipped his head as the cheers of the gathered villagers washed over him, swept across them all. Holt didn't realize he had joined the cheering until he felt the hoarseness in his throat. And then he had to agree—Sir Ira's decision was the right one.

The celebration lasted far into the night, though the weary travelers retired to their hut well before silence settled over the village. In the morning, as they woke, saddled the horses, and prepared to depart, Holt felt a wistfulness at the thought of the friend they would leave behind. Yet he also knew a profound sense of delight, grateful for the knowledge that there were places like this in Karawenn.

"Someday, when all this is over, we'll be back to see you," he told Sir Ira.

"You—all of you—shall always be welcome," replied the owl. "And know, too, that you'll be missed."

Danis sniffed back a tear as she tenderly embraced the owl, who sat upon Lancer's saddle for perhaps the last time. Led by Gallut, the party filed through the mostly slumbering village and the pastoral forest beyond.

The big centaur led them at an easy walk along a wide, sun-dappled trail. The gently rising pathway meandered through the forest so gracefully that it seemed almost level.

Only after they had ridden for an hour, traversing most of Riftvale, did the Daryman look behind them. He was startled by how far they had risen—the village was a tiny sprawl alongside the stream, far below, while the narrow crack through which the companions had entered the valley now vanished into the distance. The opposite wall of the circular depression seemed a smooth, seamless cliff.

"About the wall . . . tut, tut—it's a shame we had to break it," Tellist Tizzit noted.

"We'll repair it immediately," Gallut declared breezily. "Now that we have a king, *anything* is possible!"

Finally the centaur drew up before the foot of the precipice marking the far edge of the vale. A tumble of boulders lay strewn before them, but there was no sign of any gap. Holt was surprised when the big centaur leaned down and, with a rippling of the sinew in his arms and shoulders, lifted a large boulder out of the way to reveal a narrow, shadowy mine shaft.

"Go here," he said. "Beyond you will find the heights of the Wyrmrange."

Immortal Game

"Thank you," Danis said. "Your aid has been valuable to us all."

"Can you tell us how large the mountain range is?" Fenrald wondered.

Gallut shrugged. "No one has been to the top of the crest," he said. "And who knows what lies beyond?"

With these ominous words ringing in their ears, the companions dismounted and entered the narrow, low-ceilinged tunnel. Tellist Tizzit led the way, casting a light spell that glowed from the palm of his hand, shedding cool illumination through the darkness. As soon as Fenrald, in the rear, had entered, the centaur rolled the boulder into the gap behind them.

For hours, the companions pressed through cool dampness, grateful for the wizard's light. The tunnel was narrow for the most part, but quite solid, shored with timbers and several sturdy stone arches.

"Gnomish digging," Fenrald declared, nodding in approval. "But it's interesting that they made it high enough for humans—or even centaurs. These folk really do work together."

In several places, the excavated tunnel passed through larger, natural caves, and Holt was awed by the icicle-like spikes of rocks that plunged downward from the ceiling, or rose in mirror image upward from the floor. Then the passage became again a narrow corridor, and the company shuffled along in claustrophobic anxiety.

The tunnel ended, plugged by another large boulder that Fenrald and Holt were barely able to muscle out of the way. Pushing forward, anxious to emerge into daylight again, the Daryman stepped through the opening and promptly halted in shock, appalled by the landscape that greeted his eyes.

The other companions emerged behind him, until the entire party stood upon a high mountain ledge, a shelf barely wide enough for them all. Below, a sheer cliff plunged away, while all around soared peaks more craggy, more barren and forbidding than anything he had ever seen.

"These are bigger mountains than the Trollheights, that's sure," Fenrald muttered, trying to overcome his own disquiet. He harrumphed skeptically. "Not so cold, though."

Indeed, the wind that washed across them was thick and uncomfortably warm. A strong smell of sulphur permeated the air, and the sky overhead was leaden with clouds as dark and oppressive as smoke. Remembering the tales of mountains that spewed fire into the sky, Holt wondered if the air was in fact filled with the stench of these unimaginable flames.

They worked their way along the high slope. Fenrald—because of his mountaineering experience—now took the lead. The pathway was clear, and the group finally descended to one of the barren valley bottoms.

"It's amazing a place like Riftvale could be hidden here," Danis said, looking wonderingly around. "Everything about these mountains seems so bleak, so dead."

"Not totally," Fenrald demurred. He pointed to several trickles of water, fringed by greenery. "There's water here, and it's pure enough for moss and bushes to grow. Still, it looks pretty desolate—that I'll agree with."

"Where'll we camp tonight?" Holt wondered, realizing that a sheltering forest grove would be very hard to find.

"Cave, maybe—or under the stars," the dwarf replied with a shrug.

Holt looked upward at the roiling, smoky sky, and was not very optimistic about seeing any stars. As his eyes swept across the jagged horizon, he glimpsed a flash of movement on one of the upper slopes. He stared at the place for several minutes, but made out no more motion.

Still, as he turned his eyes toward the forward trail, he could not shake off the feeling that something lurked there—something with hot, hungry eyes.

As he rode along, Holt imagined he could feel those eyes boring steadily, dangerously, into him.

10
Felicia

Holt poked through the low brush on the valley floor, unable to find a branch even as thick as his thumb. Many twigs were brittle and dry, but would flash into ashes within a few moments after lighting. Shivering against the dark night, he trudged back to his companions.

"We'll have no fire tonight," he announced glumly.

"That's fine with me. I'm too tired to hold a stick over the coals anyway," Danis groaned, lifting a loaf of hard bread and a small slab of salt pork from her supplies. "How about cold supper—and as much sleep as we can get away with?"

As Holt settled into his bedroll, he found himself missing the contented hoots of Sir Ira's snores. The Daryman slept with the Lodestone Blade in his hand, and when Syssal awakened him shortly after midnight, he felt as though he had barely closed his eyes. Together with Fenrald, he spent the next hours staring into the gloom, against a night that seemed darker and more dangerous than any Holt had ever known.

Smoldering dawn probed at last through the dense, unnatural overcast. Saddling Old Thunder, Holt suddenly glimpsed a shadow of movement high on the mountain. He squinted, scanning the high, steep slope, but saw no further sign of anything alive there. Remembering his earlier suspicions, he resolved to remain alert.

That day the travelers progressed along the floor of a narrow, cliff-bracketed valley. In places, the passage tightened to a virtual gorge but always progressed upward, sometimes steeply. In these places, the companions were forced to dismount, leading the skidding, frightened horses up sliding inclines of loose stones.

Gradually the valley curved toward the right. The face of the mountain beyond rose in a series of dark, unclimbable shoulders and jutting cliffs of slick black rock. Only the floor remained passable, leading onward and upward. At every bend in the trail, Holt worried they would discover an impassable cliff, or the tangled wreckage of a landslide that would completely block the path.

At last the valley walls swept outward, revealing a notch against the smoky sky. Scrambling and sliding, the companions crested the last steep incline to reach a narrow saddle nestled between two massive mountains. The summits to either side were so huge that even the greatest of the Trollheights would have been dwarfed in the shadow of even one of them.

Immediately below the climbers, the mountainside plunged away, descending a long, steep slope until it vanished into a murky haze of shadow. Holt saw a reflective ribbon, undoubtedly a stream, gleaming through the mist. Beyond the hazy valley rose a nightmare landscape, and the Daryman shook his head and blinked, reluctant to believe that the vista was real.

On the far side of the vast gorge rose a ridge. Beyond jutted a mountain that looked as though it had been rended by some mighty immortal hand. Once the summit must have risen in a vast cone, for the lower slopes of the great peak circled symmetrically, all sweeping upward toward a single point. Yet that point was no longer part of the mountain. Instead, the upper third of the peak was gone, replaced by a smoldering crater. The companions couldn't see into that vast space, but red light flickered along the rim, pulsing upward with a surreal, powerful illumination.

"Heads up!" cried Fenrald in alarm.

The Daryman drew his sword, spinning and looking upward, astonished. Dozens of creatures bounded down the slopes of the flanking mountains. Giant ratlike attackers scrambled from both directions, bouncing on all fours toward the pass, growling and snapping with each agile leap. The nearest of the monsters sprang onto the rocks looming overhead, and Holt saw the pointed nose, the wicked and glittering eyes. These were wererats, identical to the creature Whisktale had become.

One of the huge lycanthropes leapt toward the Daryman, but he cut it down with a slashing chop of the Lodestone Blade. Danis struck another shaggy flank, her sword glistening red as she drew it away from the dying wererat. Fenrald's magical hammer soared out and crushed one of the monsters before circling back to the dwarf's hand. Again he put the weapon to deadly use, and another wererat fell, while Syssal fitted silver-tipped arrows to his bow, shooting one of the hideous creatures after another. But it seemed that two leapt forward for every one they killed, and more and more of the snarling beasts swarmed into view.

Meanwhile Tellist mumbled something, scratching his head as he sought to recall an incantation. Suddenly a great cloud of thick fog billowed through the pass, obscuring attackers and defenders alike. "Drat!" declared the wizard, coughing and waving his hands before his face. He shouted another word, and the fog disappeared.

In the sudden clarity, Holt saw two wererats, jaws gaping, bound toward him. Long, sharp teeth glowed pale yellow, slick with drool, and the Daryman tumbled to the side, slashing desperately with his sword. One of the beasts fell with a yelp, but the other spun around and chomped those wicked teeth into Holt's left arm. The Lodestone Blade struck again, as deadly on the backswing as on the fore, but the Daryman groaned as fiery agony shot through his elbow and shoulder, seeming to wrap cold fingers around his heart. Straining for breath, he sat down heavily.

Tellist shouted something else, pointing at the nearest of the werebeasts. Bolts of magic exploded like crackling arrows from his fingertips, slashed into the monster, and quickly dropped it in a blast of blackened fur. The wizard turned his barrage against another wererat, and when that one fell, the other creatures backed away, hissing and spitting in fear.

Red eyes gleamed hatefully, but when Fenrald and Danis rushed forward, brandishing their deadly weapons, the monsters turned and ran along the mountainside. In seconds the last of the hideous, hairless tails had disappeared.

"Holt!" Danis cried, appalled to see blood running down the Daryman's arm.

He sat and nodded groggily, struggling against pain and revulsion. Quickly she made a bandage to wrap the wound and stanch the flow of blood.

As the princess tended him, Holt caught Syssal Kipican's eyes and saw that the elf frowned in dire concern. "What is it—is the bite poisonous?" Holt asked.

"No . . . not exactly," Syssal replied, his tone grim. "But werebeasts carry their disease in their mouths, and it is not unknown for the victim of a bite to become infected."

"You mean—that *I* could become a wererat?" demanded Holt. He shook his head and refused to believe what he heard.

Syssal made no reply.

"Let's get to the stream, clean it off as best we can," urged the princess. They looked down the vast and shadowy slope, unable even to clearly see the bottom. Still, there was no other choice.

The companions slipped and slid downward. The horses were reluctant to follow and frequently had to be coaxed. Led by the steady examples of Old Thunder and Lancer, however, the other steeds skidded and stepped tentatively along.

The shadows thickened as they continued their descent, but gradually Holt discerned the rippling froth of a narrow stream trilling through the bottom of the steep-sided valley. His arm throbbed, and he stumbled downward in a daze, unaware that Fenrald had taken Old Thunder's reins from his hands, that Danis held his good arm and aided his groggy, uncoordinated slide. Rocks tumbled into the stream as the companions approached the rough, rocky bank.

"Watch!" hissed the dwarf, suddenly hefting his hammer.

Holt spun, fumbling for his sword, trying to penetrate the shadows with his blurry vision. His arm throbbed, and he tried to ignore the pain, knowing he must remain alert and ready to fight. Yet his legs seemed like rubber beneath him. It was with gratitude that he felt Danis's shoulder supporting him. Leaning weakly, he allowed her to help him to a sitting position on a rock—though he kept his right hand clamped around the hilt of his sword.

"What is it?" Syssal demanded, nocking an arrow and staring in the direction of Fenrald's gaze. Holt still couldn't see anything through the darkness.

"I saw something—or some*one!*" the dwarf declared. "You there—show yourself!"

For moments, nothing happened. Still the Daryman could see no sign of a threat. The rushing of the stream was the only sound, but the dwarf's eyes proved more keen than the human's as Fenrald spoke again. "Come out from behind that rock—don't make me come and get you!"

The menace in the burly warrior's voice was palpable to Holt—and, apparently, to someone else as well. A short, slight figure emerged from behind a large boulder, and the companions gasped as the form hobbled into view.

A female dwarf limped forward, and the bruises on her round-cheeked face were visible even in the twilight.

"Help!" she cried, limping closer. "Can you help us?"

"Help who?" Danis asked. "I just see you."

"It's my village—Pumice," she said. "We're besieged!"

"What happened to you?" asked Fenrald, his voice tight with outrage.

The dwarf woman's face was swollen and discolored, with dried blood trailing downward from the corner of her mouth. One eye was puffed almost completely shut—yet the other glared with the belligerent determination Holt had commonly seen in the eyes of Graywall's dwarves. Clearly the foe that had assaulted her had not defeated her—it had only made her mad.

"It's a long story," the stranger said. Her eyes turned to the bloody bandage on Holt's arm. "What about you?"

"Our companion was bitten," the princess said, as they lowered Holt to the ground. "Come over while we tend him."

"My name's Felicia," the dwarf explained, hunching down to join the others in looking at the Daryman's wound. "And Pumice is not far from here—a

day's march up the valley."

"Pumice—never heard of the place," declared Fenrald Falwhak. He scowled threateningly, but Felicia met his gaze with a bold challenge.

"I've never met a dwarf who's heard of everything there is!" she retorted. "But that must be the case where you come from."

"No—I—I'm sorry." Fenrald backed off quickly. "Tell us—who's besieging your village?"

"The rat-men. They took this whole valley—maybe you saw some of them up above."

"Aye," Fenrald growled. "Saw many—killed more than a few."

"First came the dragon," the dwarf woman explained with a shudder of remembered horror. "Xtan is his name. He is pure evil, bringing only destruction. Like a nightmare, he swept from the sky, breathing fire, striking with his terrible claws. In minutes, he had burned the outer portions of Pumice, killed everyone he could catch. The survivors fled into the tunnels."

Holt's arm stung as though it were being consumed by fire, but though the rocklike grip of agony still clenched him, he forced himself to listen to the dwarf's tale. Even through his own pain, he felt the horror and grief brought by the dragon's attack.

"Every dwarven town has a lot of underground space," Fenrald explained for the benefit of the others. "Comes in handy for defense. But against a dragon . . . ?"

"Many of my village mates still lived," Felicia continued. "But within an hour, the rat-men came, scores of them, and now they're guarding the caves. The dwarves are barricaded inside, trapped by the wererats. No one can get out!"

"And how did you escape the siege?" asked Syssal Kipican.

"I was up on the mountain, chasing the sheep that had spooked that morning—probably because they sensed the dragon was coming. A couple of the rat-men sneaked up on me, but they're dead now. Anyway, I could see everything that happened, but they couldn't see me. After everyone barricaded the tunnels, I took off down the valley. At first I was just trying to save myself—but then I thought maybe I could find someone to help us."

"I think you have!" Fenrald declared grimly, hefting his hammer.

"Yes!" Holt agreed, wincing against the pain that flared in his arm—but fully determined to help. The other companions, too, quickly agreed.

"First thing in the morning, you take us to Pumice—and we'll scatter these rats like the vermin they are!" pledged the dwarf of Graywall.

Holt leaned back, picturing the task through the fog of his pain. They could do it, he knew—brave companions, all, with a potent sword and the spells of the wizard to help them! They could break the siege of Pumice!

Then, of course, they would have to worry about the dragon.

11
Pumice Besieged

At least the valley was warm, Holt thought as the companions huddled on the bank of the stream, settling in for another long night. Knowing that wererats lurked nearby, none of them felt sleepy. Syssal roamed around the perimeter of their small camp, keen elven eyes searching the darkness beyond.

Only Tellist fell quickly asleep. The aged wizard snored softly, clearly exhausted by the trek. Fenrald flipped his hammer in the air, catching the handle and immediately tossing it again, trying unsuccessfully to control his agitation. Beside him,

Felicia sat quietly. She had borrowed the First Daughter's hairbrush, and now stroked her long tresses, working out tangles and revealing an auburn sheen of soft curls. Even in the dim light Holt saw the dwarf woman's bright, lively eyes, and the determined set of her firm chin.

"How's the arm?" Danis asked, seemingly for the hundredth time. She settled beside the Daryman, and he welcomed her presence with a sigh.

"It doesn't hurt so much," Holt replied, taking her hand in his. He was surprised to find that what he said was true. "The swelling's gone down quite a bit, and it hasn't started bleeding again."

"Good—I don't think we'll find an inn for you, if you have any thoughts of staying behind like Gazzrick did!"

Chuckling wryly, the Daryman nevertheless sensed the underlying truth of her words. They looked in silence at the vista of jagged peaks fully encircling their deep valley. Smoke spewed from many of the mountains, and in the fading daylight, other summits glowed with pulses of crimson, as if they could barely contain their massive internal fires.

"It didn't used to be like this," Felicia declared, pointing up to the high peaks of the range. "A year ago, cool breezes flowed along here, and grass was lush in the lower valleys."

"What happened?" asked Fenrald through a jaw clenched in outrage.

"Many things," she replied, pointing beyond the ridge that now blocked their view. "The biggest mountain—Skyspire, we used to call it—had been rumbling and smoking for decades. It finally exploded. In other places vents opened in the ground, and poison gases came out. A whole village of humans was wiped out that way. Rivers and lakes boiled away, and the overcast settled across the sky. It's been more than a year since we in Pumice have seen the sun."

"Is yours the only village left—of anyone?" asked Holt. He knew of Riftvale, of course, but that place didn't even seem as if it were part of this nightmare landscape.

"As best we know. Not only did the mountains become our enemies, but they also gave birth to the one who would seek out every living thing to kill or enslave. Those villages, those peoples spared by quake and eruption, fell victim to an even greater horror—the dragon."

The Daryman grimaced as he remembered the ruins of the gnomish city and tried to imagine the killing power of such a beast.

"His name is Xtan, they say. Huge as a moraine, he is, and as red as blood. Each of his claws is a sword mightier than any dwarven blade—yet his talons are not the most horrifying of his weapons. When he exhales his fire, Xtan slays dozens of men or dwarves in an instant. The heat of that blaze can melt stone, leaving only ashes behind."

The companions were silent. Holt fought a rising sense of despair, unable to vanquish his stark fear. How could any mortal stand against power like that? If the beast turned its eyes toward the settled lands, toward Vanderthan or Rochester, who could stop it? Even the power of wizards would be helpless before such might!

"You mentioned humans," Danis said to Felicia. "We haven't seen any sign of them."

"There *were* villages of humans throughout the range. None of them survived, so far as I know. The dragon got some, earthquake and lava got others. And some of 'em—I guess you already know—well, they *changed*. They're not humans anymore."

"All the wererats . . ." Holt couldn't finish the horrifying statement, but he fully realized the truth.

Felicia nodded grimly, leaving the Daryman's ominous words hanging in the air. Unspoken was the fear that crackled between them all—would his own wound infect him? Would Holton Jaken succumb to the deadly disease?

"Lycanthropy, it's called," Syssal said grimly, his back to the companions as he continued to study the night. "It affects different peoples in different ways. Fenrald or I, for example, would probably find it fatal—we of the elder races possess a resistance to lycanthropy that is deadly in its ultimate victory."

"But humans . . . ?" Danis left the question

148

incomplete.

"I have heard it said that if the disease takes hold, it is not uncommon for a human to *wish* that the effects were fatal," the elf noted, his tone grim. He looked at Holt frankly, and the Daryman sensed the regret, the plea for understanding in his friend's expression. The human forced himself to listen to Syssal's awful words, believing that the more he learned about the danger, the better he would be able to battle the infection—or at least, to recognize the onset of its effects.

"Tut, tut . . . the results are far from certain, you know," Tellist Tizzit declared, sitting up and stretching his creaking limbs. "It's not a sentence of doom—necessarily."

"The wizard is right," Syssal agreed. "The disease takes a varying amount of time, I understand, before the effects are evident. For some, it's a few days; for others, as much as several weeks. No one can say for sure with any particular individual. It's often tied to the cycles of the moon; however, after the affliction has taken full possession of a victim, it's possible for the cursed one to change shape at any time—day or night, new moon or full."

"That attack at the Catfish Inn occurred under the full moon," Holt remembered. He looked up at the universal overcast, unable to discern any brightness through the thick layer of cloud.

"We're four days, maybe five, away from the full moon again," the elf said quietly.

"You mean—that I'm going to turn into one of those rat-creatures?" Holt tried to comprehend the threat, told himself that he should be terrified. Yet for the present the idea was almost too bizarre to horrify.

Syssal nodded grimly. "It's possible. And if you did, you would be a grave danger to all of us."

"Surely I wouldn't turn on you—not my friends!" The Daryman shook his head stubbornly. "No disease could make me do that!"

"Simple transformative reaction, actually," Tellist Tizzit explained, as if he were describing the magical conversion of salt into sugar. "The human is devoured, as it were, by the lycanthrope. You would no longer be Holton Jaken, Daryman of Oxvale—instead, you would become a wererat, fiend of Entropy!"

"Tellist!" snapped Danis.

"Oh, dear," gulped the wizard, as if he had just heard his own words. "Well, I'm sure it's not as bad as all that. Perhaps you'd be just a minor fiend, not really nasty at all—"

"It will not happen!" Holt's tone was so grim that the others fell into silence. "I'll resist this disease—our quest is too important for any weakness!"

Privately, as he finally drifted toward sleep, the Daryman made another pledge. *If* he began to show signs of infection, if he saw any indication that he would in fact succumb to this dire malady, he would do whatever was necessary to make sure he didn't endanger his friends.

In the morning, Holt's wound had healed remarkably well. Only a reddish scar remained, and he had no swelling or unusual discomfort. Shortly after first light, they were off, Felicia and Fenrald in the lead, guiding the companions toward the hidden site of Pumice.

The mountain village occupied a series of ledges high on the wall of the valley, the dwarf woman explained. Its location had protected it from assault until the time of the dragon, when Xtan landed on the largest ledge and belched his killing breath onto the outer portions of the town. In the confusion caused by his fiery arrival, the wererats had scrambled up the steep approach paths. Only because of their steady nerves—and the heroic courage of a few valiant and doomed defenders—had the bulk of the dwarves been able to flee into the underground portion of the town.

"Those paths leading upward are all in clear view of the village—and all the open plazas were watched by rat-men, last time I looked," Felicia explained. "I think it's best we take the long way."

She led them up a steep and narrow trail that switched back and forth across the valley side. The sun penetrated the hazy overcast, pouring shimmering, broiling heat onto the laboring adventurers. Still, they continued upward, finally reaching a high crest where the trail leveled out. Felicia walked out along a ridge that was barely five or six feet wide. Canyons plunged to either side, and rippling, jagged-crested massifs rose beyond the chasms. Once again, the smoldering crater of Skyspire was visible. Though the trail was smooth, the travelers continued to lead their horses, as if fearful an extra few feet of height would prove too disconcerting.

"We'll wind around this next mountain," Felicia explained, pointing toward a summit that rose from the crest before them. "From there, we can approach Pumice without being seen."

"Unless they have a guard on top of the cliff," Fenrald cautioned.

"Do you think they'd think of that?" she wondered.

"No sense taking a chance—I'll go ahead and have a look."

As they worked their way around the shoulder of the mountain, the slope rose steeply upward to the right, but still plummeted in a long descent to the left. Fenrald jogged ahead, his hammer loose in his hand. As he rounded the obstruction, he carefully climbed down to the rocks below the trail, making slower progress when he advanced but remaining concealed from any watchers.

The others halted, and nearly an hour passed before the dwarf came trotting back into sight— this time on the trail.

"There *was* a wererat standing guard, but no

more," Fenrald said grimly. Holt saw that the dwarf's hammer had been newly cleaned, and imagined the fate of the monster. He almost felt a twinge of pity for the creature as they resumed the advance.

"Just over the crest here," Felicia said.

Before them, the trail dropped out of sight, and they cautiously approached the edge. Leaving the horses under Tellist and Syssal's control, Danis, Holt, and the two dwarves crept to the brink of the precipice and looked down. Holt immediately saw the body of the wererat guard. The creature had been bashed in the head and now lay on a ledge just below the top. The Daryman crawled to the side in order to avoid the gruesome remains and get a clear view of the village.

The upper terrace of Pumice was no more than a hundred feet below. The shelf was a long, narrow ledge on the mountainside, dotted with the same square courtyards and blocky stone buildings that characterized Graywall—though Holt saw immediately that this town was nowhere near as big as that teeming city. Charred roofs, splintered walls, and scattered stones all marked the damage inflicted by the dragon; the Daryman gulped in awe as he considered the strength necessary to wreak such havoc.

Several figures scuttled around the town— wererats racing here and there on business that seemed to drive them into a frenzy. A dozen or more of the creatures, however, squatted watchfully beside the wall of the cliff.

"They're guarding the doors," Felicia whispered.

Beyond the first terrace, the lower balconies were barely visible. None of them seemed as wide as the upper level. Dust and dried leaves swirled across the farther surfaces, but Holt saw no sign of wererats below the higher plaza. After studying the town for several minutes, satisfying themselves that they had located most of the wererats, the companions backed away from the ledge to make their plans.

"That big group of them is gathered in front of the tunnel doors," Felicia explained. "The others seemed like they're just patrolling, or looking for mischief."

"How can the few of us break the siege of a whole village?" Danis asked.

"The biggest liability for my fellow dwarves is that the gates are sealed now, from the outside," explained Felicia. "As long as the dragon doesn't return, we'll free the village if we give them the chance to get out and help us."

"You think the dwarves in the tunnel will charge out when we attack?" Holt asked.

"Sure they will!" Fenrald declared. "All we need to do is give them the opportunity."

"Before I fled, I saw the wererats nail beams against the outer doors. The first thing we'll have to do is knock those aside."

"A job for a hammerin' dwarf, I'd say," suggested Fenrald, "once the wererats are out of the way."

"Perhaps I can clear the way before the doors," Tellist Tizzit suggested. "A fireball should scour the ground of these scum."

"Can you be sure the fireball goes where you want it?" Holt asked nervously, remembering a few of the wizard's more colorful magical mishaps.

"Tut, tut—such a lack of faith," chided the mage. "Of *course* I can! It's the spell itself that sometimes proves a little hard to remember. Let's see, now—how did that go again?"

He mumbled to himself as the others finished their plan. "I'll stand with the wizard and use my bow," Syssal declared. "My sword will be ready if the fighting gets close."

"Good," Danis said. "The rest of us can stick together, going in with our blades."

"Just be careful with that fireball!" Holt reminded Tellist, who was still muttering to himself.

Tingling with nervous energy, Holt led Danis and the two dwarves down the twisting road toward the village. They crouched low, sometimes crawling to insure they couldn't be observed from below. The elf and the wizard took up position on a high overlook while the other four crept to the edge of the village, taking shelter behind a low stone wall. Peering cautiously, Holt saw the heavy doors, and the sturdy beams that had been erected to hold them shut.

"What's taking Tellist so long?" wondered the Daryman. They waited for several minutes in growing agitation. Holt was on the verge of starting back up the road when they heard the unmistakable chanting of the wizard's spell.

Immediately a jabber of alarm rose from the wererats crowded on the terrace. The creatures scuttled from the charred buildings, gathering before the gates into the mountain, gaping upward with alarm. Several raced toward the roadway where Holt and his companions lay concealed.

A tiny marble of light drifted downward, weaving erratically through the air before it dropped into the midst of the gathered wererats and vanished. Holt's heart sank—Tellist's spell had failed, altogether!

Abruptly, flame flashed through the town, and a billowing cloud of roiling fire exploded upward, roaring like an angry furnace. Wererats screamed, briefly, as they were engulfed by the killing blaze. The oily tongues of crackling heat licked outward, reaching around the buildings, pouring over the stone walls, and clearing the space before the gates.

Shrieks of unspeakable pain and horror rose in a wild din as burning wererats leapt and writhed on the stone plaza. Holt watched in horrified fascination as several of the flaming monsters raced toward the precipice and hurled themselves into the deep canyon.

Many of the monsters—including those who had started for the upward road—escaped the fire. They howled in fury, sprinting and bounding forward. Red eyes glowing, the monsters snapped rat-like jaws and growled, slashing wicked talons amid a cacophony of hissing and snarling.

Holt and Fenrald sprang into the roadway, Danis and Felicia close behind. The Lodestone Blade cut down the first of the lycanthropes while the dwarf's hammer smashed into another. More monstrous attackers pressed forward, and for several desperate moments the four companions stood against a press of growling, snapping wererats.

Dropping an enemy with a deft stab, Holt turned to parry the attacks of another wererat—but that one fell dead, pierced by an arrow from above. Nearby, Danis fought with cool fury, blocking and chopping against two attackers. She was forced to step backward, but when Holt leapt to her aid the two humans quickly dispatched both drooling brutes.

"Charge!" cried Fenrald, leading the companions into the burned-out area before the tunnel doors. His hammer whirled out, dropping a wererat as the creature scuttled toward the lip of the precipice. The weapon returned to him as usual, flipping back into the dwarf's hand, and he immediately turned to the stout logs that had been crudely braced before the doors. With several powerful smashes, he knocked them aside.

"Dwarves of Pumice! We're rescued! Charge!" cried Felicia. She pounded on the beams with her mace, helping Fenrald clear the way.

Immediately the portals swung open, and dozens of stocky, bearded warriors rushed forth, loudly bellowing their desire for vengeance. Swords and axes waving, beards bristling in the fury pent up during the siege, more dwarves exploded outward from the tunnels.

They were led by an imposing, gray-bearded fellow who wielded a massive axe, clutching the haft in both of his hands and slashing the weapon through deadly arcs. His helm trailed eagle feathers, and his long arms extended as the keen axe blade sliced through one wererat after another.

"Follow me!" Holt cried to Danis.

The two darted along the edge of the terrace, catching a wererat and cutting the creature down as it lunged toward escape. A swarm of the monsters charged, and for a moment, the two humans fought back to back, carving deep wounds in any wererat bold enough to close. Soon the dwarves of Pumice reached them, and moments later, the last of the nearby lycanthropes had been slain.

Quickly the dwarves and their allies rushed to the lower terrace, where they found a few wererats hiding among the bins and barrels of a storeroom. These, too, met a swift and merciless end. Charging onward with Holt and Fenrald in the lead, the

Douglas Niles

vengeful dwarves raced to the lowest terrace, but found no sign of their enemies.

"Looks like the last of 'em," the dwarf muttered in disgust as they saw the naked tails of several wererats disappearing around a bend in the trail. The terrified creatures didn't look back as they raced toward the valley floor below.

"Not many got away," Holt said with satisfaction. The attack had been sudden and brutal, and they had carried the day without suffering further injury. He felt a flush of triumph and elation.

"Nope—not many," the dwarf said in a tone that quickly tempered Holt's fierce delight. "But even one of 'em is enough to go get that dragon."

With this sobering knowledge in the forefront of their minds, the two companions turned back to the village. They climbed up to the middle terrace to meet their new allies—and to plan for the next onslaught of Entropy.

12
Council in the Wyrmrange

"By all the Spheres, Felicia—I feared I'd never see you again!" cried the grizzled dwarven warrior who had led the charge from the gates. His hair and beard matched the gray color of his weathered steel battle-axe. From the dwarf's silver armbands and the tufted crest of eagle feathers on his battle helmet, Holt judged him to be some kind of chief. He spread his muscular arms wide, folded the young dwarf woman into his embrace, and released a long, ragged sigh of relief. "I–I can't believe you're alive!"

"These are the ones who made it possible," Felicia told the venerable fighter. "Travelers in the Wyrmrange, and enemies of Entropy." She embraced Fenrald with an arm, and the other companions with a sweeping gesture.

Turning toward the companions, she explained. "This is Dargan Greataxe. He's the chieftain of Pumice—and my father."

She introduced the three humans, Syssal, and Fenrald to the misty-eyed dwarf, who shook each hand with crushing force. "Never thought I'd be welcoming an elf to my village," Dargan said with a scowl that quickly melted into sincere gratitude. "But for your help this day, I can only offer my thanks."

"The choice was simple—no choice at all, really. Your daughter makes an eloquent ambassador," Syssal Kipican replied.

"Aye—she's a good speaker, she is," agreed Dargan.

"And handy with an axe, I'll witness!" Fenrald declared. The dwarf's face was bent into an odd expression, which Holt suddenly deduced was blissful happiness. Fenrald's eyes sparkled as he smiled at Felicia.

The dwarf woman lowered her own gaze. "Fenrald comes from Graywall," she explained. "He's a battle chief over there."

"We've heard of that grand city," Dargan declared. "It's a wish of mine to see it someday."

Fenrald cleared his throat and stood straight, speaking as an emissary of his realm. "In the Troll-heights, we heard rumors of other dwarves in Kar-awenn, but, alas, we never ventured this far from home to find out. The loss is all of ours, it would seem."

"No time better than now that we meet," Dargan Greataxe declared, his tone growing grim. "I fear that the very survival of Pumice is at stake—with implications for all of Karawenn beyond!"

"The dragon. . . ?" Holt inquired.

"There are many threats, in truth, but aye—the dragon most of all."

The Daryman turned his eyes toward the darkening sky, studying the smoldering stratus, seeking any glimpse of movement in that expanse of shadow. In places, the underside of the cloud glowed pale crimson, and reflecting the fires of some deep gap in the surface of world. The dragon could be soaring through that overcast, and they would never see it until flaming death engulfed them.

"Er, tut, tut—given that same dragon, perhaps it would be prudent for us to go inside," Tellist observed, sharing Holt's apprehension.

"Good idea." Dargan Greataxe led the companions and his own warriors back through the heavy doors into the underground portion of his town. Holt looked at the massive slabs that formed the gates, which were currently illuminated by torchlight. Each was more than a foot thick, hewn timbers of giant trees strapped together with massive bands of iron.

Once inside, Holt began to feel a little more encouraged. Like Graywall, Pumice seemed to have been designed with defense in mind. The corridor inside the gates extended straight into the mountainside. Holt saw narrow slots in the ceiling over their heads, and knew that dwarves could gather in the upper chamber and pour arrows, hot oil, or other attacks down upon any invader. Shortly the passage twisted and forked, and each turn was a strong point where a lone dwarven warrior could hold a number of attackers at bay.

They reached a large central chamber, circular in shape, with a high, domed ceiling. A fire crackled on a broad, central hearth, the smoke sweeping upward and away through a hole in the dome. In this audience room, Dargan led the companions to a long table, and they all took seats together with several of the town's elder dwarves

"Our chieftain spoke the truth when he discussed our danger," a dwarf who had been introduced as Baltan Silverhaft declared. This grizzled fellow wore a dark, silver-embroidered robe that drooped all the way to the floor. From the amulets and feathers draped around his neck, Holt recognized the dwarf as a powerful shaman. "We fear that Entropy surges against the world itself. There are fires breaking through the ground everywhere—as the whole land collapses. The dragon is Entropy's potent agent, but even if Xtan does not destroy us, the melting of Karawenn will."

"It's Entropy on an unspeakably grand scale," Holt said quietly, drawing the attention of the others. He thought of the mountains exploding, landslides and eruptions wearing away the very ground beneath their feet. "The world collapses, destroyed by fire from within." The Daryman thought of another threat of Entropy—the disease that even now might be eating at his very being.

Baltan Silverhaft seemed to read Holt's mind, for his next question was directed at the human. "You were wounded on the arm—bitten by a were-rat, I see. But not today?"

"The wound was yesterday," the Daryman admitted, examining the mostly clean bandage wrapped around his forearm. "How could you tell?"

"I have trained many decades to see things that evade the mortal eye," explained the dwarven shaman.

"Do you know—is there a cure for the disease?" Danis inquired.

"I have heard that such a curse can be removed, with faith and diligence. Alas, such healing requires the powers of a cleric much greater than I. Still, the force of Entropy is not irreversible."

"Sir Ira! Perhaps *he* could—" Danis spoke up hopefully.

"He's not here!" Holt declared forcefully. "And

besides, we have to forge ahead. This danger to me means next to nothing compared with the threats to all Karawenn!"

"Tut, tut—not that the whole world would be destroyed," Tellist cautioned. "Most likely just the greater portion . . . Er, I suppose that's not terribly encouraging, is it?"

"No—it isn't," Danis sighed. "And I wonder how much of the danger is connected to . . . our mission."

"We dwarves—well, we're private folk," Dargan said awkwardly. "I have no wish to pry into the matters that bring you to the Wyrmrange. But know this: if there is any way we can help you fulfill your task, you have but to ask. Anything that lies in our power shall be yours."

"Thanks, my friend," the princess replied. She looked at Holt, and the question in her eyes was plain: do we tell these dwarves about the crown?

Without hesitation, he nodded.

The First Daughter of Vanderthan started by relating the arrival of the artifact as a blazing meteor from the sky, a little more than one year ago. Dargan immediately pointed out that the eruption of Skyspire corresponded exactly to the coming of the crown. "We saw that shooting star right before the mountain blew—always thought of it as a portent of evil," he growled.

"It is," Fenrald replied—and no one debated the point.

Danis described their wish to destroy the precious crown, and Holt and Fenrald related their efforts with fire and hammer in Castle Vanderthan, and Tellist's magical attempts in the Rocklands. Finally, the princess told of her examination of Whisktale.

"It was the wererat seer who told us—truthfully, I'm convinced—that the crown could be destroyed in the Wyrmrange."

"At the same time, Whisktale *wanted* us to come here," Holt noted. "For reasons we don't understand."

"And *how* to destroy the crown we still don't know," the princess concluded grimly.

For a time Dargan and his fellows remained silent, pondering the difficult task. It was Holt who was the first to speak.

"The summits here rise as high as any in Karawenn. Tell me, do you know what lies beyond?"

The chieftain of Pumice shook his head. "Before Skyspire exploded, it was unclimbable. Since then, we've been too busy defending our village to explore. Legends have long said that beyond the ridge all is fire—a chasm that plunges as far as the eye can see, offering naught but desolation, poison, and death."

"The fourth border of Karawenn," Holt mused. "If it's true, we live in a world held in a box. We're cornered between World's End, and the great sea—and the boundaries of rocky Trollheight and the

166

fires beyond the Wyrmrange."

"I wonder if this fiery expanse, this doomscape, might give us the means to destroy the crown," Fenrald suggested. "If we could hurl it into a chasm of purest heat, could the flames in the bowels of Karawenn melt it?"

"How can we tell?" Holt objected. "And if we threw it there, and it was lost to us but not destroyed, who's to say that some servant of Entropy won't retrieve it—and use it to enslave all Karawenn?"

"There's a way—one way only—that I might be able to tell," she said hesitantly.

The Daryman saw immediately what she had in mind. "No! Don't put the crown on again!"

"I have to—don't you see? I have to wear the crown and see if I can discern anything about our destination. Otherwise we could wander around in these mountains until winter comes and still not figure out how to destroy it!"

Her words made too much sense for further argument, but Holt nevertheless turned his face away as she went to her saddlebag and retrieved the platinum circlet. He heard her voice shaking when she asked if he would come outside with her, and for the first time he realized she feared the crown as much as he did.

Slowly, his hand resting on the hilt of the Lodestone Blade, Holt walked with Danis through the widespread portals of Pumice, onto the broad terrace

of the town's upper tier. At the low wall bordering the descent to the next level, they halted to look at the forbidding heights above. Night darkened the sky, but fiery light from within surrounding mountains still cast its sinister, pulsing glow against the underside of the dense clouds.

Above those clouds rose the moon, the Daryman sensed acutely. The alabaster orb was nearly full, and shed its compelling brightness across all the world. He couldn't *see* it, but he knew beyond any doubt that it was there.

Holt became aware that Fenrald, Syssal, and Tellist had come to stand behind them as Danis slowly raised the crown over her head. The Daryman lifted a hand as if to stop her, but rested it on her shoulder instead, willing her to have strength—not so much now, but in a moment when she would try to remove the powerful artifact.

The gleaming metal touched the First Daughter's golden hair, and immediately the impassive screen fell across her face, masked the brightness of her eyes. She shrugged Holt's hand away, but took no notice of him as she studied the high crater of Skyspire.

For a long time, she stared into the dim and smoldering murk that was night in the Wyrmrange. Bright crimson flares rose from the crater of the great volcano, silhouetting the splintered rim of the peak against the seething clouds. Gradually Danis swept her gaze along the ridge, surveying one side of the cratered peak.

"That mountain—it's dying," she said slowly. "Entropy rots within, and great destruction gathers in its bowels."

"Is that where the crown may be destroyed?" Holt asked, but Danis apparently didn't hear.

"Over there . . . we can climb to the ridge. I see a place . . . the horses will never make it. We'll leave them here. Some of you might not make it either—you'll have to try, though. There, as we go higher, there we can triumph. Or there we can—"

Abruptly she screamed and staggered backward. "No!" Danis cried, clasping the crown to her head with both hands. Holt seized her wrists while Syssal and Fenrald clutched at the artifact, but only gradually could they pry it free. When they did, the First Daughter collapsed, sobbing, into the Daryman's arms.

"What was it?" he asked after she settled down. "What did you see?"

"It was the dragon!" Her voice quavered, then grew strong. "I saw the whole way up the mountain, the path to victory, toward the end of our quest! We can reach the crest, stand upon the highest part of Karawenn—and from there we can see the means to destroy the crown!"

"The chasm of fire?" asked Holt, remembering Dargan's description.

"I don't know—I couldn't see any more details. When we got there, the dragon was waiting. Glad to see us—it *wants* us to climb the mountain!"

"Tut, tut—and what happened next?" inquired the wizard.

"The dragon opened its mouth, and I was consumed by flame," the princess declared weakly. "I was swallowed by fire!"

"By the Spheres!" Tellist declared, shaken.

It won't happen! Holt made the promise to himself, even as Danis still trembled against his chest. He pledged that, if they reached the crest as she had foreseen, it would be the Daryman of Oxvale—not the First Daughter of Vanderthan—who carried the crown to its doom.

13
Red Wings and Fire

For a time, Holt resisted the need to sleep. Instead, he paced restlessly through the halls of Pumice, talking with Danis until she retired, then seeking out some of the dwarven guards near the great iron gates. These grizzled veterans told him of the coming of the dragon, and—though each had lost bold companions and loyal friends in the horrific onslaught—their mood was not fear, but grim-faced anger.

These thoughts occupied the Daryman as, ultimately, he walked alone. Once he went to the heavy gates and looked at the leaden sky overhead. Even through the clouds, he could sense the presence of the moon . . . calling, compelling, drawing him with a dire summons.

Finally he went to a pallet provided for him in the corner of the great room, and found oblivion in several uninterrupted hours of sleep. When he awakened and emerged from the tunnels beneath the gray light of dawn, he knew the time had come to move.

Holt found Danis stroking Lancer's neck in the makeshift stable that the dwarves—who had no beasts of their own—had provided. The climb from the town would be too steep for the mounts, so the companions had arranged to leave the animals in Pumice until their return. The Daryman went to Old Thunder, feeling a poignant loneliness that took him by surprise.

"We'll be back for you, old friend," he said gruffly, clapping the big draft horse on the neck, hoping he spoke the truth.

"By the Spheres, I hope so," Danis said, clenching her arms around the neck of her faithful charger. Lancer nickered appreciatively before turning his attention back to a bin of barley that Dargan had graciously provided from the dwarven brewer's stockpile.

As they emerged from the stables, they found Fenrald talking to Felicia.

"No, lass," the dwarf said. "It would be too dangerous. But if we're successful, I promise I'll stop back here—probably before you notice I'm gone. And if we fail . . ."

"We won't fail," pledged the Daryman grimly.

Felicia clasped her arms around Fenrald and, ignoring the other companions, planted a firm kiss on the dwarven warrior's lips. His face blushing crimson above the mask of his whiskers, Fenrald stammered and huffed, but then embraced the dwarf woman warmly before they turned to the upward trail.

"Are you sure you can make it?" Danis asked Tellist, who tottered up beside her.

"Oh, posh—of course," the wizard said, looking fiercely at the trail that snaked up the mountainside, as if daring the route to speak a challenge of its own. "Besides," the elderly mage admitted with a sheepish smile, "I can always levitate on the *really* steep parts."

Syssal, his quiver stocked with fresh arrows—each tipped with a razor-sharp arrowhead of silvered dwarven steel—joined them as they made their farewells to Dargan and his clan.

"You'll have shelter here, if you need it," pledged the chieftain of Pumice.

"We're grateful," Holt replied.

The Daryman and Danis took the lead on the narrow trail, followed by Tellist and Syssal. Fenrald gave them a small head start, and then came watchfully behind. Eyes roaming across the skyline, Holt studied the far horizons, then scouted the rough and rocky terrain that spilled down from the summit and made upward progress very difficult.

Working his way among the jumbled rocks on the incline, the man from Oxvale found just the barest hint of a trail. In places, rubble fully obscured the path, and at its best, the route was no more than eight or ten inches wide. Still, dwarven engineering showed in its secure footings, and in the ingenious way that it switched back and forth across the steep face, always maintaining a steady ascent without forcing the companions to scramble on hands and knees.

The terraces of Pumice rapidly dwindled, until the broad balconies on the canyon walls looked like tiny, crescent-shaped slivers, with the cavern doors now hidden from view. In time, the rounded bulge of the mountainside blocked sight of the dwarven town, and ultimately, a wilderness of peaks and smoldering sky surrounded the companions.

Holt tried to focus on the terrain, but his mind insistently conjured images of a huge, fire-breathing dragon. His search for a tactic they might use to fight or evade the monster ended inevitably in despair. The Daryman could only hope the deadly serpent wouldn't find them—if it discovered them in the open, their quest would certainly meet a sudden and tragic conclusion.

As the companions pressed up the steep, winding

trail, Holt tried to scout potential hiding places—
and quickly realized that such shelters were rare on
the barren mountainside. He eyed the occasional
looming overhangs, examining the shady niches
underneath. Though few of these were actual caves,
even a slight shelf of rock over their heads might
prove invaluable in concealing them from a predator in the skies.

Yet, too, the Daryman found his eyes constantly
drawn to the high horizon. Never had he seen
mountains like these. Their towering majesty
compelled his attention, his awe, and his respect.
Fierce, forbidding summits tumbled everywhere
in a chaos of swells and dips, like the tempest-
tossed waters of a raging sea.

The trail continued relentlessly upward, twisting around craggy shoulders that formed short
cliffs above or below the climbers. As they worked
their way toward the ridge that formed their horizon, Holt remembered his earlier glimpse of the
splintered Skyspire. That great crater was concealed behind the crest, but he imagined it smoking and seething, awaiting their approach with
palpable eagerness.

As the afternoon waned, the Daryman considered a more immediate concern: where should
they spend the night? The few shelters he'd seen
had been tiny, with rough and rocky floors. None
had looked like a comfortable place to spend an
hour or two, not to mention a full night. The entire

mountainside was devoid of trees, and though the wind was warm, it was also strong and persistent.

Traversing a rounded curve on the flank of the mountain, the climbers came upon an even broader vista of the Wyrmrange. Peaks jutted across the horizon, while the slope before them plunged into the abyssal depths of a vast canyon. In places, a ribbon of frothing water was visible in the depths of that gorge, though frequently shelves and shoulders of rock blocked the view. Skyspire, no longer obscured, rose in blocky majesty beyond the chasm.

Nearby, Holt noticed two massive slabs of rock. Fate had toppled them together to form a makeshift tent. Wind gusted through both ends, but the broad slabs would keep any rain off their heads.

"Good spot," Fenrald agreed as he caught up to the companions beside the makeshift shelter.

"I don't want to be an alarmist—perish the very thought—but does anyone else feel a twinge of nervousness?" asked Tellist, looking around.

"What do you—?" Holt started to question the mage, but was interrupted by Syssal.

"Yes—let's get under shelter. Now!" the elf urged with uncommon forcefulness.

They scrambled beneath the looming slabs of stone, crouching in the shadows and looking outward. The whole vast canyon yawned between them and the high rim of Skyspire.

"Look!" hissed Danis, her tone taut with fear.

A crimson shape glided into view, soaring around a mountain far down the valley. Broad, leathery wings extended to catch the warm updrafts. The creature's sinuous tail floated through the air behind a massive body, and golden eyes stared unblinkingly across the mountain-scape below.

"Xtan!" Holt's voice was a barely audible hiss, echoing the knowledge—and horror—shared by them all.

Though the serpent was more than a mile away, the mere sight of the dragon caused the Dary-man's flesh to tingle in unnatural panic. He imagined the killing power of those great claws, the might of the crushing jaws. Even the horrible nightwing, a creature that had come close to slaying them all, seemed a feeble threat when compared to the monstrous menace embodied by the soaring, serpentine form.

"It's searching," the Daryman whispered, chilled further by a sudden understanding of the dragon's slow, watchful flight. The massive head swayed regally from side to side, and the creature banked this way and that to slow its glide. Always those golden eyes flashed across the ground, back and forth. Holt could sense the hunger in that gaze, and he felt his tangible fear growing hard in the pit of his stomach.

Apparently the monster was interested in lower

slopes, for it flew along the course of the canyon, gliding below the companions and never looking toward the high ridgeline. Growing smaller in the distance, the crimson serpent seemed to cease moving, to hang suspended far along the gorge of the great canyon—until, eventually, the beast dived to the side and vanished from view.

For long minutes afterward, the companions huddled in their shelter, silent and awestruck. Holt didn't realize that he tightly clutched the hilt of the Lodestone Blade until his fingers cramped. He had to pry his stiff hand from the weapon.

"How can we fight *that!*" Danis said, finally breaking the silence.

"We can't," Syssal replied.

"The elf's right—we have to make sure it doesn't find us," Fenrald stated bluntly.

"Well, this is a good place to hide—for now." Danis indicated their crude but large shelter.

The companions ate a cold supper, and Holt offered to take the first watch, since once again he didn't feel any urge to sleep. He paced restlessly outside the stone tent, probing the night with his eyes, ears, and nose. He was surprised to note the wealth of scents carried to him by the wind. The sulphurous air of the Wyrmrange was a strong blanket of stench; but other smells, of ashes, and water, and rats, seemed to poke through holes in that squelching layer.

Once again, the Daryman felt the compelling

power of the moon above the clouds—almost full, now. Perhaps one more night, maybe two, and that glorious orb would form its complete circle of brightness. What would happen to him then? Would he become a monster? No—he wouldn't allow it!

But why, then, did he feel that lunar allure?

After Fenrald came to relieve him, the Daryman lay awake in his bedroll, struggling against a sense of bleak, all-consuming despair. Only the fact that Danis slept soundly a few inches away gave him a glimmer of hope—and the courage to face the coming dawn.

The next day the climbers resumed their march, but now they were faced with a descent into the great canyon that separated them from the Wyrm-range crest.

"Felicia said there used to be a bridge at the bottom," Fenrald said, indicating the ribbon of glimmering white water flowing soundlessly far below. The dwarven trail continued down the precipice, though on this side, more and longer sections had suffered damage from gravel slides and erosion.

They had barely descended below the lip of the canyon when Holt felt an itch at the back of his neck. He scratched at the tickling irritation, but immediately knew that this wasn't a physical discomfort. Whirling around, he saw a manlike shape duck out of sight above.

"I saw 'em too," Fenrald declared, hefting his hammer. "Wererats—two or three, back there."

The same lycanthropes had served the dragon, in the attack against Pumice. Would they find Xtan now, give to the monster information about these trespassers in the Wyrmrange? Trotting along as quickly as he dared, Holt looked around for possible shelters. If the dragon caught them in the open . . .

A crack of shadow darkened the wall of the canyon a short distance ahead, where frost had splintered a narrow niche into the cliff wall. The gap had expanded from the freezing and thawing of centuries until it was several feet wide, and extended for a great distance overhead.

Holt approached the place to look inside—then stumbled backward as a red-eyed wererat leapt at his face, snapping yellow fangs and uttering guttural snarls.

Instantly, the Daryman slashed with the Lodestone Blade, and the monster retreated on its hind legs, swiping taloned forepaws at Holt's face. Black lips stretched along the monster's pointed muzzle, twisting with raging snarls. The wererat snapped again, and curved yellow fangs clicked sharply against each other.

Attacking, the Daryman feinted a wild slash before whipping his weapon around for a fatal stab. The creature slumped backward, crumpling to the ground—but still moving. Holt saw the snaky tail disappear, watched the grotesque features twist into a humanlike visage. With face filthy and unshaven, nails torn and dirty, the fellow looked like a miserable wretch—but one who had undeniably been a man.

Holt thought of whole villages succumbing to this deadly plague, and for a moment he trembled from the force of his rage. This vicious curse, lycanthropy, sent pangs of nausea through his stomach.

How could a man let such a thing claim him? The answer was obvious: If the disease gnawed away his spirit and his humanity as well as his body, perhaps it could conquer even courage and determination. But not with him. The Daryman shook his head angrily and stalked into the niche, ready to use his blade again, as often as necessary.

The cavelike shelter was empty. The passage extended inward for a great distance, and offered the protection of a descending, narrow ravine eroded by centuries of flowing water.

Returning to the trail, Holt blinked in the pale daylight that filtered through the clouds. The niche might have made a good shelter, but what was the use of that, really? He knew that they needed to keep moving.

"Dragon!"

Fenrald's shout cut through Holt's musings. The Daryman looked upward, gasped at the plunging image of a bright red body and a widespread mouth filled with wicked teeth. Xtan had broken from the dark ceiling of cloud, plummeting like a stone toward the companions on the mountainside trail.

"In here!" cried Holt, waving his hand at the rock-bound niche. "Go all the way back—keep going!"

The hair on the Daryman's neck tingled as he stared in horrified fascination at the sky. With great jaws spread wide, the vast and blood-red shape swooped straight from the clouds. It was too massive, too horrible to truly comprehend.

Holt pulled Danis by the arm, propelling her into the niche while Tellist stumbled behind and Syssal, too, glided into the shadows. The dragon was almost upon them as the Daryman and the dwarf dived headlong into the shelter of the crack.

A roar of frustrated rage shook the foundation of the mountainside. Holt, crawling frantically, felt the ground thump from a heavy impact. The monster had struck the ledge where moments ago the companions had stood upon the trail. Risking a backward glance, he saw only sky directly outside the mouth of the shelter—no doubt Xtan's momentum had carried him far down the mountainside.

But the Daryman knew with equal certainty the dragon would be back.

"Down—go in all the way," he cried to Danis

and Tellist. The shadows were thick, but the pair groped into the steep chute that water had eroded through the mountain. The cut was a long, rough-sided channel, barely three feet in diameter and descending into deeper darkness.

Quickly, the companions scrambled down the narrow ravine. All the while, Holt imagined a ball of oily, magical fire licking his heels. When the dragon returned, would the deadly breath reach them, kill them all?

The Daryman followed the others, sliding head-long, his ears pounding from the roaring of his imagination. He felt the presence of the dragon like a palpable stench in the air around them, knew that the monster had returned from its plunging dive and now lurked at the very lip of the cave.

Heat and light flashed in a surreal eruption. Flames hissed and seethed into the gap, roaring like a monstrous bonfire. Horrific sounds rumbled through the air, causing the cliff walls to tremble around them. Rocks splintered loose from the ceiling, and a pounding, rolling explosion thrummed in the mountain.

Holt crouched in terror, pressing himself against the wall, wondering if he was about to die.

For a long time, the stone resounded with the force of the fireball. The bright glow spilled into the depths of the ravine, but the blistering heat dissipated in the outer portions of the rude shelter. Finally, the fireball melted away, leaving the terrified companions sweat-soaked and shuddering.

They were safe for the moment—but, too, they were caught in a very secure trap.

14
Xtan

Though the blast of supernatural fire faded quickly, the walls around the companions remained warm, a reminder of violent death lurking immediately outside. The stench of soot and ash lingered in the air, so thickly that Holt's tongue seemed to be coated with the stuff. He wiped a layer of moisture from his brow and shook the salty drops from his hand, but his eyes stung as sweat trickled down his forehead. When he tried to shift to a more comfortable position, he felt the wringing dampness of his clothes.

The total darkness of the impromptu prison did

nothing to ease his anxiety. He heard the labored breathing of Fenrald and Danis nearby. He could only hope Tellist and Syssal were just beyond—for some reason, he couldn't bring himself to speak. None of the others, apparently, dared to break the silence, either, for they huddled in speechless misery as interminable heartbeats ticked by.

At first Holt barely noticed the illumination that ever so slightly brightened their confining shelter, but he squinted in growing concern as he saw Danis flip open the flap of her backpack. Light emerged from within, shed by the Crown of Vanderthan.

When she raised the artifact in her hands, the magical glow suffused the cramped passageway. The Daryman saw the fear plain on the First Daughter's face, and he guessed her intent—and knew the misgivings she must feel.

"No!" he objected, his voice a rasping croak. "Don't use it—don't put it on!"

She looked at him with kindness and genuine regret. "We don't have any choice—do we?" she asked.

"Let someone else—let *me* wear it!" he urged, his tone growing stronger in his desperation.

"The crown is mine—it is right that I don it now," she replied. "I—I'm sorry," she added, blinking back tears.

Then the circlet touched her scalp, and the moisture in her eyes vanished immediately. Her expression hardened—gone were regrets, fears, hesitations. Stonelike determination fell across her features like a mask, and she rose to step past Holt.

He stood and faced her, staring with awful despair into the blank, emotionless wells of her once-beautiful eyes. "Don't do this—!"

"Be seated!" she snapped.

The crown, as always, compelled obedience in those near to the wearer. The Daryman slumped to the floor, unable to resist the compulsion. Miserably he watched her scramble up the sloping floor of the chute. She moved with steady grace, climbing strongly, reaching for purchase with feline confidence. Soon she was out of sight, though the brightness of the crown lingered as a fading indication of her presence. That glow, too, slowly diminished as she moved farther from their hiding place.

Holt stood again, finding that he was no longer bound by the command she had issued.

"Be careful, lad," Fenrald said, rising behind him. "That crown might give her some protection from the fire, but the rest of us would be killed in a second if we get too close."

"We don't *know* that it will protect her!" Holt objected. "I've got to go with her!"

"We'll all go out there, see if we can help," Syssal agreed. "But the dwarf's right—we know that the artifact protects its wearer against harm. We have

188

to hope its immunities extend even to dragon breath."

"Tut, tut. From what I know of these beasts, they can only breathe their fire a couple of times—then they're limited to their teeth and claws until they rest up again," Tellist said brightly. "That should give us some hope!"

Holt remembered the massive fangs and talons of the serpent, and did not feel terribly encouraged. And even one more blast of that horrific breath would slay the princess if the crown was not as potent as they hoped. Yet he started upward, blindly following her—and as he climbed, he grasped a truth about himself. If Danis Vanderthan perished, he himself would have no reason, no desire, to keep living.

Daylight filtered into the niche, lighting the final portion of his scrambling ascent. A shadow blocked the entrance to their shelter, and then Danis was gone, moving quickly and smoothly. While she wore the crown, fatigue and soreness would have no effect on her, though he himself was gasping from his frantic efforts to catch her. He heard sounds behind him as the other companions also followed.

When he reached the entrance to the niche, he saw Danis already a hundred yards from the opening, marching boldly down the trail. Beyond the princess, coiled into a bundle of scarlet scales sprawled across a broad, flat-surfaced shoulder, the dragon watched her approach.

In repose the creature seemed even more massive than when he had first attacked. The wedge-shaped head, as big as a rowboat, rose slowly on a rippling, snakelike neck. The wyrm's reptilian visage was set with bright yellow eyes that gleamed with intelligence—and pure, calculating evil. The crimson tail lashed back and forth as huge leathery wings unfurled slightly, ruffling in a menacing display. Unblinking, the dragon watched Danis advance along the trail. The great head tilted downward on the curve of neck, still towering above the First Daughter as she continued her measured approach.

Then the dragon spoke in a voice that boomed and echoed from of the surrounding heights. "Why do you come to my mountains, human? Do you seek my treasure, like all the other petty thieves? To do so is to die!"

"We seek no treasure," Danis replied in a formal and commanding tone. "We are travelers, desiring only to pass."

"Gentle lies, my lady," the dragon mocked. Tilting his neck forward, he blinked and squinted slightly. "And a pretty lady you are . . . pretty, and bejeweled—but a fool."

"I am no fool," Danis warned.

"But for coming here, to the mountains of Xtan, you *are*," the serpent replied with a chuckle that rumbled through the ground.

Holt, creeping slowly along the trail, heard the menace in that sound and trembled so much that he had to crouch in place and grit his teeth against a wave of instinctive fear.

"I travel where I will upon Karawenn," the princess replied. "I mean you no harm, nor any thievery—but you shall not bar me from passing."

The icy tone of her voice almost matched the dragon's.

Xtan didn't laugh this time. "I have important matters to attend," he declared. "Affairs across the breadth of this world you would travel so lightly. I grow tired of your tedious prattle."

The dragon's jaws abruptly gaped, and a massive, billowing cloud of fire roared outward in a rushing, expanding ball. Flames of orange, of yellow and white, bloomed and hissed in the air, engulfing Danis and masking her completely. A sound like a raging furnace filled the air, and the Daryman's own cries of horror were lost in the din. The heat of the fire down the trail washed against his face and arms—but he couldn't look away, couldn't shield himself from that impossible nightmare.

As quickly as they had begun, the flames faded, leaving a smoldering patch of ground. Amid tendrils of wispy smoke stood the First Daughter of Vanderthan—to all appearances unharmed by the inferno. Holt stumbled to his feet, lurching down the trail toward Danis. The Crown of Vanderthan gleamed on her head, and she planted her hands on her hips as she met the dragon's look of surprise.

"Interesting," Xtan declared. "How can it be . . . ? Yes! By the Spheres! It's *you!*"

Abruptly, the wyrm frowned in a grimace of exposed fangs. Leaning forward, blinking those cruel eyes, he stared at the princess—or rather, at the top of her head.

"There it is!" Again came that evil laugh, and Holt had never heard a more chilling sound. Still he crept forward, the Lodestone Blade in his hand. Neither the dragon nor Danis took any notice of his approach—he might have been an insect to them, for all the intensity of their mutual concentration.

"Whisktale was right. You have brought it here, to me!" Xtan leered, his expression growing even more cruel.

Halting behind a large rock, Holt felt an acute helplessness. The dragon's eyes remained fixed on Danis. The crown's protection wouldn't extend to Holt—if the dragon chose to breathe fire again, he would be killed if he got too close.

Xtan lunged, reaching both forepaws to encircle Danis. The princess didn't cry out, didn't make any sound, but her steel long sword flashed against the dragon's talons. Hissing furiously, the wyrm reared back and bashed Danis with a heavy blow, knocking her through the air. She tumbled, rolling along the trail while her sword spun out of her grip and skidded down the mountainside.

Holt charged from behind the rock, Lodestone Blade in hand. If he could just get close enough, could strike a deep blow against the serpent . . . The notion seemed ludicrous even as he thought it, but he had no choice.

The dragon pounced, catlike, after the tumbling form of Danis. One massive forepaw pinned her, and then Xtan plucked the princess off the ground. Her head flopped downward, but still the crown remained in place on her scalp, the artifact's power holding it there.

Then she moved, and Holt's heart leapt—Danis was still alive! She squirmed in the creature's grip as those vast wings extended and pulsed downward to drive a wash of wind into the Daryman's face. The princess locked eyes with Holt, and he was shocked by the cool appraisal in her expression. Danis looked up at the dragon, saw the wings driving faster, then twisted back to regard the man.

Holt croaked an agonizing cry as the monster leapt from the mountainside, pulling upward with massive wings. Roaring in helpless fury, the Daryman flailed at the creature flying high overhead. The princess of Vanderthan squirmed and struggled in Xtan's huge forepaws.

"Holt!"

Danis's voice, shrill with terror and urgency, cut

through the roar of wings. She held the crown in her hand—and when she removed it, the full horror of her circumstance must have struck with appalling force.

The Daryman sprinted along the trail, following beneath the dragon as he carried his precious victim higher and higher into the sky.

Silver winked against the seething clouds, and Holt saw the thing tumbling through the air, knew immediately what it was. His first thought was despair: without the crown, Danis had no hope against the omnipotent wyrm. Yet the Daryman sheathed his sword at the instant of recognition and reached out with both hands to catch the artifact. The magical metal stung his hand when it struck. He held it with loathing, barely restraining the urge to cast the hateful thing away.

Then he looked skyward, trembling as he watched the blood-red form of the serpent shrink into the distance. He couldn't see Danis any longer, but the dragon's foreclaw was still clenched.

Tellist, Syssal, and Fenrald joined Holt there. They watched, unspeaking, until the flying wyrm vanished around the looming ridge of the highest mountain in the world.

15
Canyon and Summit

Holt looked at the artifact he still clutched with white-knuckled intensity. His eyes turned back to the sky, but there was no longer any sign of the red dragon, nor of its helpless captive.

"I'm going after her," the Daryman said.

"We're with you, lad," Fenrald pledged.

Tellist and Syssal nodded grimly. Delaying only long enough for Holt to bury the crown in the depths of his backpack, the companions started down the trail into the canyon.

They descended the steeply inclined pathway, pressing along the treacherous trail with reckless haste. Ignoring their aching knees and the increasingly raw blisters burning their toes, the four desperate companions hurried downward, Holt setting a pace that was almost a run.

Syssal kept up without difficulty, but Fenrald fell behind, despite the fact that his legs were pumping furiously. The dwarf was breathing hard, wiping sweat from his sodden brow. Tellist Tizzit was even farther behind, his face drawn, his breaths coming in deep, rattling gasps.

Biting back his impatience, Holt slowed.

Shadows already cloaked the deepest part of the chasm, though it was only two hours past noon when they arrived at the bank of the river. Here they found the bridge that Felicia had remembered—or at least, what was left of it. The span was mostly gone. The remnants were just a pair of sagging cables, marked by splintered remnants of boards, swaying dangerously low.

"We can cross—but it'll be tricky," was Fenrald's immediate assessment.

Holt wondered if the dwarf painted too rosy a picture. The bridge had once been suspended by four cables, but the two on the right had snapped. The remaining pair drooped in parallel strands, one about three feet above the other. The lower cable trailed into the water for a dozen paces of its length. A few of the boards that had once formed the bridge surface dangled loosely from the lower cable, but most of the planks had already vanished into the torrent.

"Balance your feet on the lower wire and hold onto the upper with your hands," the dwarf suggested. He looked at Tellist Tizzit and hesitated.

"Tut, tut—a bit too dicey for me, I'm afraid," declared the elderly mage. "I think I'll just teleport myself across the river and meet you on the other side."

"We're going to climb the trail across the canyon," Holt said. "Why don't you teleport all the way to the top and wait for us there?"

"Splendid idea—splendid!" Tellist agreed, eyeing the daunting precipice on the far side of the river. The trail switched back and forth up the slope, extending far beyond their view. "Tut, tut—it's true I'm not as young as I used to be. I'll be waiting for you on the top."

"Good." Holt was in fact relieved that they wouldn't have to worry about the wizard making the precarious crossing or the strenuous climb—though, as always, he worried about a possible mishap in Tellist's spell. "But be careful!"

"Naturally, my boy, naturally. Now, let's see, a pinch of this . . . how did that chant go again?" The wizard's voice trailed off as he scratched his white-whiskered chin.

"I'll go first," the Daryman offered Syssal and Fenrald, and he started toward the twin cables.

"Wait—let's lash this around you. Just in case," Fenrald declared. He extended a loop from the coil of rope he wore around his waist, and the Daryman tied himself to the line.

Meanwhile, Tellist began to mutter something, staring upward as he sought his intended destination. In the middle of a word, the wizard blinked out of sight, and with a soft popping sound, air rushed into the space he had vacated.

"D'you see him?" asked the dwarf, squinting up the cliff across the river.

"No." Holt shook his head, trying to bury his misgivings. "We just have to hope he made it. Are you ready with that rope?" The dwarf nodded, and the Daryman stepped onto the lower cable of the ancient bridge.

The strand swayed under his weight, and he grasped the upper cable, straining to maintain his balance. By leaning backward, he found that he could lever the two cables apart with his body, providing at least a minimal balance. Sliding his hands along the upper line, he stepped sideways, moving out from the stony riverbank until he was above the deep, roiling water of the channel.

He cast a quick look back to Fenrald, and saw that the dwarf had braced his feet and was firmly grasping the other end of the rope tied to Holt's waist. Gritting his teeth, the Daryman progressed over the dark and angry current. The cable sagged under his weight, and as he neared the middle of the river, water rushed over his feet, and then his lower legs. The liquid was as warm as fresh blood, and Holt looked down to convince himself this was indeed a mountain stream.

Maintaining his grip against the pull, he strained to hold his balance. In the center of the river, his legs were submerged to the thighs, and the current was a powerful force, striving to push him into its flow. As he loosened one foothold, the water pressure surged against his hips, sweeping his other boot off the heavy cable. Grasping with his hands, Holt let his body extend, his legs and torso pushed downstream. Struggling to hold against a force that seemed to double or triple his weight, the Daryman pulled himself sideways until he could again draw a foot up and brace on the lower strand, with just his sodden boots underwater.

Grunting in desperation, sweating amid the steamy spray, he at last crawled off the cable on the far side of the stream and collapsed on the rocks, weak from fatigue and fear.

Yet they had no time to waste. Together with Fenrald, the Daryman secured the rope for Syssal's crossing. The elf used the twin cables, relying on the rope as an emergency support. Because he didn't weigh as much, the lower line didn't drop so deeply into the water, and Syssal was able to make the crossing without incident. The elf and the human then braced the end of the line for Fenrald, who was also able to cross without slipping, though he cursed and sputtered when the water came to his waist in the center of the river.

"What about that dragon?" asked the dwarf as he sprawled beside his companions on the bank. "By now he's sure to have figured out that he doesn't have the crown."

"I think he must be waiting for us to bring it to him." The bitterness of Holt's tone didn't conceal the fact that he believed what he said. "He's got Danis—and he knows we'll come for her. He'd rather have us deliver the crown to him than take the chance of losing it again—what if he comes after us, and we manage to throw it into the river, for example?"

"Could be," Fenrald remarked skeptically. "One way or another, it doesn't change what we've got to do."

"Another thing—the dragon said something about Whisktale," Holt remembered. "What do you think that meant?"

"Could be that the rat-fellow is here, somewhere," admitted Fenrald.

The elf nodded in agreement. "At the very least, he's been in touch with the dragon."

"Too bad we couldn't kill him in Rochester," Fenrald growled.

"It may be that we'll still get the chance." Holt's hand tightened around his sword as he thought of the horrid lycanthrope. With a shudder, he recalled the beast's transformation before their eyes, and forced himself to ignore the possibility that such a fate might lie in his own future.

"Let's go, then," suggested Syssal, climbing to his feet.

They rested only long enough to catch their breath, not bothering to dry their sodden garments before they started up the far side of the canyon. The steep incline was at first a relief from the grinding descent. Now, at least, toes were spared the pressure that had given them blisters, and the soreness of creaking knees was alleviated by pressure on hips and heels.

Thick shadows shrouded the trail, masking the river below and the continuing slope above. The three climbers paused often to gasp for breath, but none felt any desire for longer rest. The image of Danis Vanderthan imprisoned in the dragon's lair was too horrifying to allow for any delay. Soon, they had fresh blisters growing on their heels, and fierce aching racked every joint.

Of immediate concern to Holt was the fear that they might miss Tellist, in case the wizard had found a resting place somewhere slightly off the trail. The afternoon brightened as they climbed higher, light seeping in subtle gray through the heavy clouds, a gloomy illumination showing the vast canyon sides like the forbidding walls of some monstrous castle. The climbers continued, moving through the realms of pain into total numbness, placing one foot before the next on the basis of instinct more than conscious thought.

The incline lessened as the three weary companions drew near the upper reaches of the canyon. Now the river was out of sight below them, and the trail switched back and forth through regions of looming cliffs and narrow, twisting ravines. Pausing for breath in the shelter of one of these ravines, the Daryman leaned against an outcrop of rock—then sat up straight, startled by a tentative voice he heard from below.

"Er, is that you, Holton?"

"Tellist!" cried the Daryman, leaping to his feet. He stepped to the edge of the trail and looked downward. Staring up at him from perhaps thirty feet below were the watery eyes and rounded spectacles of the wizard. Tellist stood upon a narrow ledge, facing the cliff and clinging with both hands outstretched—as if he attempted to wrap the whole, vast mountainside in an embrace.

"Tut, tut—you're a sight for sore eyes, I must say. Can you possibly drop me a rope?"

"Sure—but how . . . ?" The Daryman's question trailed off as he guessed. "You teleported up here, but missed the top of the cliff by a few feet?"

"Purely bad luck, I assure you," the wizard replied. "Except for that minor detail, the spell couldn't have worked better. Saved me no end of blisters and sore muscles. Though I must say, I'm fortunate this ledge was here!"

"You've been there all afternoon?" asked the dwarf in amazement, quickly lowering his looped rope.

"It would have been quite a vantage, actually, if I had been facing the other way," Tellist declared breezily. "I'm quite rested—ready to get on with the march!"

In a few moments, they managed to get the end of Fenrald's rope to the stranded wizard. Tellist tied the line around his chest, and the others hauled him up to join them. With an "oof" and a "tut, tut," the mage untied himself, dusted off his loose robe, and pronounced himself ready to travel.

Relieved to have their companion back, the four questers started along the trail again. They soon crested the final walls of the canyon and worked toward the top of a vast, domed ridge. That elevation formed one of the approaches to the crater of Skyspire—the great mountain where Xtan and Danis had disappeared.

As they neared the long ridgeline, Holt wondered what they would find beyond. For the long weeks of their approach and entrance to the Wyrmrange, this height had been their distant horizon—the edge of Karawenn. Would they discover another bottomless well like World's End? Or more, even loftier heights rising to the heavens themselves? Might they see the chasm of fire about which the dwarves of Pumice had spoken, a crevice where the crown might be destroyed?

Brown fur and red eyes flashed from behind a looming boulder, and Holt clutched the Lodestone

Blade in his hand, cutting down the first wererat before he even realized they had been ambushed. In moments, dozens of the snarling, snapping brutes erupted from concealment, charging toward them from all sides.

Fenrald dropped another with his hammer while Syssal drew his own sword, disdaining bow and arrows in these close quarters. Snarls echoed everywhere, and Holt heard the now familiar snapping of wererat jaws.

Tellist muttered a spell. The sparkling traces of his magic missiles arced and sputtered through the fight.

The leading wererats veered around the Daryman, having learned to fear that gray stone blade. Holt leapt at the flank of one, killing it with a swift stab before he whirled to face another that pounced behind him. That one also went down, and the Daryman searched for the next foe, barely aware of the battle fury that had settled over his mind.

He rushed toward a pair of wererats that snarled and lunged at Tellist. The Daryman shouted, drawing the monsters' attention from the wizard. They leapt, but with two quick stabs, Holt killed both.

Nearby Fenrald was backed against a high boulder, battling three of the brutes. Holt sprang to the dwarf's aid, driving the lycanthropes back and fatally slashing one, then another.

The Lodestone Blade seemed to have a will of its

own, a desire to seek and slay the monstrous rats everywhere. The Daryman's mind seethed and churned, cloaked in a haze of battle. Slashing, stabbing, thrusting, he whirled this way and that, cutting into wererats on every side. He hungered to strike down these hideous beasts—even to cast away his sword and bite the creatures with his own teeth!

Gradually the haze fell away from Holt's eyes. Staggering weakly, he shook his head and blinked. Dimly he recognized his surroundings: he stood with his companions in the midst of nearly two dozen corpses—many of them ragged-looking humans. Other felled foes were still undergoing the grotesque transformation back to their human bodies.

"That was some fight, lad," the dwarf declared, awed. "You could have saved a few more of 'em for us," he added in a gruff attempt at levity.

"I–I don't know what happened to me," the Daryman replied. "It was as if each one of these beasts were standing between Danis and me—and I had to remove them."

Or was it something darker? a voice wondered deep inside of him . . . some animal power growing, swelling near the surface, ready to explode with the might of Entropy?

He remembered something else. "Do you think one of these brutes was Whisktale?"

Fenrald had been looking over the gory remains,

and he shook his head. "Can't say for sure, but I don't think so."

Syssal looked away from the battleground, studying the heights. "Now, where do we go?"

"Still upward," Holt replied, turning his eyes toward the crest. His momentary madness unsettled him deeply, and he found his hands clenching involuntarily as he resumed the climb. Nervously he looked at his fingers, seeking any sign of claws, or bristling hair. He reminded himself that lycanthropy could claim him at any time. Had his rage been inspired by that dire force of Entropy? Or was it a symptom of his own struggle to defeat the scourge?

Scrambling up the last hundred feet before the ridge, Holt was suddenly eager to see beyond this barrier. The first thing he noticed was that the sky brightened perceptibly in the distance.

In another step, he reached the horizon and paused in surprise. Of all the things Holt had imagined, he wasn't prepared for the vista that greeted them.

"An ocean," Syssal declared, joining the Daryman to look at a sweeping expanse of placid water. The mountains plunged to a shore many thousands of feet below. From there, sparkling blue water extended to the distant horizon—perhaps a hundred miles or more away.

The clouds that lingered over the Wyrmrange broke beyond the water's edge, and the sun-dappled expanse of sea was smooth, rippling with gentle swells. There were no angry whitecaps, no sweeping currents like those beyond the mouth of the Tannyv. Brilliant colors—emerald at the shoreline, aquamarine along the shoals, and indigo in the deeper waters offshore—glowed in the sparkling expanse, and far away, the rugged outlines of green, mountainous islands rose from the glimmering sea.

"Karawenn doesn't end here!" Holt's awe softened his voice. "It goes on . . . how far?"

"Can't say. But we've learned that there *is* no chasm of fire," Fenrald noted, shaking his head. "No place to throw the crown."

"No—not below," Holt admitted. "But the crown *can* be destroyed here; we just haven't found how."

"But we've found something else," Syssal declared.

Holt turned to follow the direction of the elf's gaze. His eyes came to rest against the lofty mountain that grew out of the crest of this ridge. On the side of the peak, well below the crater, they saw a tiny spot of darkness in the distance.

Syssal didn't need to elaborate. Holt, Tellist, and Fenrald all had the same thought as the elf. They looked at that dark aperture, so high and aloof from the world, and they understood.

They had found the lair of the dragon Xtan.

16
Guardians
of the Lair

The top of the lofty ridge was broad and rounded, surfaced by small, loose stones, and only gradually sloped. It made for easy walking—especially when compared to the long, draining ascent out of the chasm.

Holt's feet advanced without his conscious thought, avoiding the larger rocks and carrying him steadily upward.

Though the rim of the crater dominated the landscape before the Daryman, he found himself glancing wistfully to the vast, placid sea beyond.

The water sparkled like diamonds, late afternoon sunlight spilling from the clear skies above the ocean. The mountain's ashy clouds glowered immediately overhead, but the reflected glare of the sea had an invigorating effect on the climbers. The expanse of water looked immeasurably peaceful, and Holt found himself wishing he could embark with Danis in a sturdy boat, raise a sail, and leave this tortured realm behind.

Though his thoughts rambled through such diversions, his eyes were drawn inevitably back to that shadowy spot on the high summit. Staring back at them, malevolent and dark with menace, the cavern mouth was the opposite of the placid sea—a dark, unblinking eye of purest evil and insatiable decay. It seemed that all the power of Entropy was centered in that single, black, emotionless hole.

Over the course of several hours' walking, the company climbed steadily. The sun dipped toward the horizon, streaking the underside of the clouds with curls of smoky lavender and orange fire. The cave remained high above them, not appearing to get any nearer, only larger.

"It's huge," Holt declared, voicing the opinion shared by them all. The gaping hole in the mountain loomed high, dwarfing the rock formations that bracketed the opening.

"Certainly big enough for the dragon to fly into," Syssal agreed.

"D'you suppose he's waiting right inside the entrance?" growled Fenrald suspiciously, hefting his hammer in clear readiness to face the serpent on the spot.

"Tut, tut—let's not be impatient. I suspect that's a pretty deep hole, and dragons like dark places. They need plenty of rest. He's probably sleeping somewhere near the center of the mountain."

Tellist's reassurances notwithstanding, Holt kept his eyes on the entrance to the dragon's lair. The terrain grew steeper as the ridge merged into the high mountain itself. The companions climbed around a steep knob of barren rock, and then the cavern entrance loomed like a black, gaping mouth before them. They had finally reached it. In the extending shadows of twilight, the lair stood out like a spot of perfect blackness, as dark as the dragon's heart.

"Do you think there might be traps—or guards?" worried Tellist Tizzit.

"Could be," Fenrald mused.

"Should we . . . what should we do?" whispered Holt.

Only then did the Daryman realize the others were watching him, waiting for him to say something. For a moment, he felt lost, looking to Fenrald for advice, wishing Sir Ira or Danis were here. But in the next instant, he shook back his worry and nodded firmly.

"All right. I'll advance into the lair first. The rest

of you, keep an eye on me."

Holt stepped toward the cavern mouth, and then looked back at his companions. He was surprised at the twinkling lights in the clear sky over the ocean, and realized these were the first stars he'd seen in many nights. Pausing for a moment, he stared in wonder at the distant celestial display. At the same time, he felt the summons of the full moon, still concealed by clouds, but wide and luminous in the lofty sky. He looked toward the obscured horizon, knowing that the orb had just risen—and profoundly frightened by the fact that this was such a strong and precise awareness within him.

For the first time in the Wyrmrange, Holt felt a chill. Wind blew landward from the vast sea. Despite the goose bumps raised on his skin, the Daryman relished the fresh air that pushed back the sulphurous breezes.

He turned his eyes back to the lofty summit, shrouded in the shadows of overcast, darkened by nightfall. "Let's go," he said quietly to himself, with a grim sense of purpose he knew his companions shared.

Squinting through the shadows, the Daryman studied the dark mouth of the cave. Its upper lip loomed far overhead—the gatehouse of Castle Vanderthan could stand inside the opening without touching the ceiling!

He advanced into the lofty vault, ignoring

cramped and stiff muscles, grown energetic in desperation. The others followed. The ground was clear of obstacles, smooth enough to let them walk with ease. Syssal and Fenrald, whose night vision was much more keen than the humans', soon took the lead. They picked as soundless a path as possible.

Holt looked back, seeing the star-speckled entrance diminish behind them. A few moments later, a slight curve in the tunnel's course had altogether blocked the opening from sight.

Holt set his free hand on Fenrald's shoulder, trusting his companion's keen eyesight to discern a safe route. At least the floor remained smooth—despite the darkness, Holt didn't stumble or make any untoward noise. Occasionally a deep, sinister rumble would rise from the depths of the mountain, echoing through vast caverns and resounding from side passages that the Daryman couldn't see. Nothing but sound, Holt told himself. Nothing but sound.

They pressed farther in, beginning a long descent into realms of rock that grew warmer and more sulphurous with every step. The wide passageway twisted through several graceful curves, leading ever downward, into the smoldering heart of Skyspire.

A high ceiling loomed overhead, and as Holt's eyes gradually adjusted to the almost perfect darkness, he discerned occasional passages opening to either side. Sometimes fresh air wafted from these huge connecting tunnels; others exuded a stink of rot and decay.

"See—*there!*" hissed Fenrald suddenly, drawing Holt's attention to a shadowy rock formation before them.

"What?" he wondered, whispering as he crouched beside the dwarf.

Fenrald pointed to a patch of dark shadows before the looming formation.

"Manticore," breathed Syssal, barely making a sound. The name meant nothing to Holt.

Pulling the two humans behind the shelter of a boulder, the dwarf explained in hushed tones. "I saw it pacing back and forth."

"What's a manticore?" whispered the Daryman.

"A natural killer, that's what. As big as a lion, and it loves to eat flesh. It can fly, too—but the worst thing is the tail."

"Why's that?" Holt wondered, clutching the hilt of his sword. He found the prospect of battle oddly exhilarating, and had a hard time standing still. The stench of the manticore came to him now, a vaguely feline odor that roused the hackles on the Daryman's neck. A snarl rose in Holt's throat, and he swallowed the urge with a sudden disquiet.

"The tail shoots spikes that are as deadly as arrows—and the manticore can launch a whole barrage at once. We've got to take it fast."

"Perhaps a light spell would help," Tellist said. "I

could blind the creature, and at the same time give us a good look at the target."

Holt was concerned about the risk of magic. "What about alerting the dragon?"

"Tut, tut—I told you before, he's probably down in the heart of his lair. And if he's not, he'll know we're here as soon as we attack. A little illumination's not going to give us away."

"You're right," conceded the Daryman, hungry for battle.

"Excellent plan, then" Fenrald agreed. "Or at least as good as we've got. I'll be ready with my hammer—"

"And I'll have an arrow ready to shoot, signalled by your spell," added the elf.

Holt drew his sword, resting the cool blade across his knees. He said nothing, not trusting his voice to remain calm.

Creeping as close as they could using the cover of the rough ground, the companions advanced to a clump of boulders a few dozen paces from the irregular formation. From there, Holt got a glimpse of the manticore. The creature was huge, muscular, feline. Giant wings riffled darkly as it turned, pacing slowly across the breadth of the tunnel, wheeling with regal grace to reverse the stately march. The rumbling growl of deep, measured breathing was audible.

Abruptly Tellist's voice broke the stillness of the night, and the monster responded with a chuffing snarl. Bright light shot through the cavern, beaming from a tiny pebble that Tellist had enchanted and then cast on the ground. The manticore spun and reared on its hind legs, the growl swelling into a roar as it regarded the glowing stone.

Leathery wings extended from the feline shoulders, and the monster's vaguely human face split in a roar, revealing a mouth filled with long, curved fangs. A black mane, bristling and fierce, surrounded the grotesque face. The manticore blinked against the brilliant light, lashing its tail, trying to find the source of the attack.

Silver flashed as Fenrald's hammer flipped outward to bash the monster's flank. The weapon rebounded toward the dwarf's hand, and Syssal fired a pair of arrows in quick succession. Each of the missiles struck the shaggy, dark pelt, and the manticore whirled, snarling in the direction of the new attacker.

Sprinting around the boulders, Holt darted toward the monster from behind. He saw that horrid tail, the tip a ball of bristling spikes, lash out. Several of the spines shot free, striking loudly against the rocks concealing the other companions. Still unobserved, the Daryman rushed closer, stabbing the Lodestone Blade deep into the manticore's side.

With a convulsive whip of that awful tail, the monster twisted around, smashing Holt with a big paw and knocking him down hard. Gasping, still

216

clutching his sword, the Daryman pulled the weapon free. The monster fell heavily to its side and uttered a gurgling, final exhalation.

Holt was about to call his companions forward when he heard another growl in the shadows. A second manticore lurked in the cave! Crouching, Holt squinted—now *he* was blinded by the light spell, and the monster had the advantage of concealment and darkness. Staying low, the man backed away from the glowing pebble, trying to see into the shadows.

He heard a clatter of sharp spines striking rocks, and Syssal Kipican groaned in sudden pain.

"Tut, tut—oof!" gasped Tellist Tizzit. The sound was followed by a crash into the boulders, and then all became ominously silent.

"There, lad—watch it!" cried Fenrald.

Holt threw himself to the ground, grunting as he felt a sharp pain in his left arm. Angrily, he seized the spine from the manticore's tail, pulled it out, and cast it aside.

Twin yellow eyes glared balefully at him from the darkness, and a leonine body crept forward. A silver object whirled past Holt as Fenrald's hammer crunched heavily into the brute's shoulder.

The manticore ignored the threat of the dwarf, raising that bristling tail over its back and advancing steadily toward the Daryman. The monster's deadly spikes jutted upward, and the tail lashed back.

Holt scrambled to his knees, helpless to shield himself.

With unfaltering courage, Fenrald charged, a stocky figure racing from the darkness. He drove the hammer against the manticore's head, and spines clattered wildly into the shadows. Swiftly, the dwarf drew back his weapon for another blow, but as quickly as any cat, the monster spun, slashing with a talon-studded forepaw. Fenrald went down like a straw dummy, tumbling over the rocks before coming to rest, motionless, against a large boulder.

But that sacrifice gave Holt the chance to spring to his feet. Snarling in fury, holding his sword extended before him, the Daryman charged the manticore and hacked savagely through the tawny pelt. He felt rather than saw the flash of the monster's darts past his head. One of them nicked his ear, but so sudden had been his charge that most of the creature's barrage went wild. Hearing the missiles clatter into the stones behind him, Holt stabbed again, driving the blade toward that snarling, hateful face.

The manticore reared back, wings flapping, and then swiped with a great forepaw—but the human was too quick. Holt met the slash with the point of his blade. The monster stepped farther backward, stung. Deep growls rumbled from that lionlike chest as the creature circled warily, hateful eyes fixed upon the swordsman. With a sudden pounce, it leapt. Holt sprang desperately to the side, landing on his feet in a fighting crouch.

This was the opening the Daryman sought. Off balance, shaking its wounded paw, the manticore momentarily ignored its pesky foe. Holt charged in, stabbing with all his might through that broad, sinewy chest, driving his weapon into the creature's evil heart. With a shuddering groan, the monster slumped to the ground and lay still.

For a few seconds, Holt stood over the carcass of his enemy. Blood pounded in his ears, and he could hear nothing over the roaring heat of his own fury. Then, gradually, his head cleared, and the pounding rage melted away.

"Fenrald . . ."

The dwarf blinked, sat up, clasped his head in his hands, groaned, and then pushed himself to his knees. Seeing that his old friend was for the most part all right, Holt turned toward the clump of boulders where Syssal and Tellist had been sheltering.

The wizard was seated with his back against a flat boulder. Both of Tellist's hands were clamped around his thigh, and Holt saw a manticore's barb jutting from the mage's leg.

"Tut, tut," muttered the wizard absently. "To let it sneak up on us from the side like that—unforgivably careless! I don't know what I was thinking!"

Since the mage didn't seem to have suffered any wounds beyond that one puncture, the Daryman knelt beside Syssal Kipican. The elf was motionless, and Holt's heart swelled with grief as he counted no fewer than three of the vicious barbs jutting from Syssal's back. Leaning close, he was relieved to hear that his friend still breathed, though raggedly.

"How're they?" asked Fenrald, limping over to the others.

"Best have a look at our elven friend," Tellist replied before Holt could answer. "I've got just a pinprick here, but he hasn't moved since he got hit."

Holt pulled at one of the darts, relieved when it came free with only a little twisting—and grateful Syssal remained unconscious. In short order, he and Fenrald had the other two barbs removed, and they stanched the bleeding with rags torn from their clothing.

The elf recovered consciousness while they wrapped the bandages, and though Syssal was white-lipped with pain, he squeezed their hands in gratitude. Holt winced at his friend's gasps when the human finally pulled the wrappings tight.

At the same time, Tellist bandaged his own wound with strips torn from his robe. He climbed to his feet, but was unable to move without leaning on Holt's or Fenrald's shoulder.

"Let's continue on—a bit, at least. Maybe find some shelter," groaned Tellist. The wizard sagged against the Daryman, and Holt knew that the mage wouldn't be able to go far.

"We'll find someplace safe, near here—a place where the two of you can get out of sight," pledged the young man.

"In here," Fenrald urged, pointing to one of the side alcoves. "You and Syssal should be able to hide while Holt and I go after the First Daughter. I don't like the thought of leaving you here. . . ."

"Tut, tut—we'll be safer than you, I daresay. Now, let me see. . . ." The wizard tottered into the alcove, leaning against the wall while Holt went to help Fenrald with the badly injured elf. Propping Syssal between them, they half carried, half dragged him into the shelter.

"Look at this!" Tellist declared brightly as they limped up to him. "I found a door!"

Holt couldn't see the outlines of the portal, but somehow the wizard had in fact located a concealed entryway. He poked and prodded for a bit, and abruptly a massive stone facade swung soundlessly inward.

No light entered the room beyond, yet a dim glow suffused the chamber. The illumination, Holt realized with sudden awe, emanated from the precious objects within.

He saw glowing coins, and a shield that cast a soft, yellow light. A rug was coiled on the floor, and several bottles of clear liquid stood against the wall.

"A treasure chamber!" the Daryman declared,

awed.

"Perhaps even secret from the dragon's own allies," Tellist noted. "It's the kind of thing Xtan probably keeps to himself."

"It's as safe a place as any to leave you," Fenrald declared. He knelt and unrolled the small carpet, finding that it was just the right size for Syssal. "Here—lie down on this."

Tellist located a padded cloak and used it to cushion himself. After making the pair as comfortable as possible, Holt and Fenrald closed the door to the treasure room. Each checked his weapon, making sure it rested securely at his belt.

Then, side by side, the two companions continued into the depths of the dragon's lair.

17
Into the Dark

"Just a minute," Holt whispered after he and Fenrald had advanced a few dozen paces into the yawning cavern.

The dwarf halted, holding his hammer, straining to see through the shadows while the Daryman shrugged out of his backpack and opened the flap. Holt carefully checked the contents, making sure the crown was secure in his bedroll. On a sudden impulse, he unwrapped the artifact and set it atop his other belongings before closing the pack and hoisting it to his shoulders.

Again they resumed their measured advance.

The floor remained smooth underfoot, the passage wide, illuminated by a glow that filtered dimly from somewhere before them. The Daryman saw numerous columns along the shadowy edges of the tunnel, and at first he thought these had been constructed by some long-forgotten builder. As the pair moved closer to one wall, however, he saw that the pillars were of natural origin. Some rose, cone-like, from the floor while others descended like icicles from above. In places the upper and lower formations joined, forming slick shafts extending from ceiling to floor.

Holt's heart ached with fear for Danis. He couldn't bring himself to believe she was dead. Somewhere, somehow, she was—she *had* to be—alive! What terror had she felt when the dragon carried her into this tomblike dungeon, beyond any glimpse of the sky?

The human and the dwarf kept their weapons raised and walked lightly downward. A dim glow began to tinge the cavern—a reddish, smoky haze, growing brighter with each step. Holt was able to make out a few details now, recognizing yawning openings to the sides, discerning the rhythmic pulse of fire from somewhere ahead of them. These intermittent moments of brightness were brief, but—like lightning flashes on a dark night—they provided clear glimpses of the surroundings.

The pair crept cautiously around a wide bend in the corridor, and stopped. Ahead, ember-tinted lights burst upward from the ground. The sparking tracers rose up from a gaping crevasse that cut across the cavern beyond, completely blocking their passage.

Together the pair crept up to the edge of the chasm. The stone-walled crevasse was too wide to jump. At each side, it merged into the smooth and seamless walls of the cavern, offering no way around. Both edges of the chasm were precipitous cliffs plunging straight into the depths. Far below, a river of crimson lava radiated waves of relentless heat. On the opposite side of the gap, a rock column spanned from the ceiling to the floor.

"The dragon flies across here, obviously," the dwarf remarked in bitterness, pointing to the wide space to one side of the stony pillar. "But I don't know how we're going to get across—unless you can figure out a way to grow wings!"

"No," Holt muttered in despair. A part of him wanted to fling himself over the brink, counting on his desperation to carry him all the way to the far side—but he discounted that suicidal idea as soon as the urge arose. "Your rope—can we use that somehow?"

"I don't see how we can fasten it over there," Fenrald growled, as frustrated as the man. The dwarf gestured to the stone column across the chasm. "If that was a stalagmite, we could lasso it. But as it is, we'd have to get the rope around the thing and bring it back—and I sure don't see how we're going to do that."

"If Sir Ira were here, he could carry it," Holt said futilely.

The dwarf, in a moment of kindness, bit back his sarcastic response.

"Your hammer!" Suddenly the Daryman had an inspiration. "Can you tie the rope to the handle, then throw it over there and bring it back to your hand?"

"Hmmm—never tried anything like that, but it's as good an idea as any," Fenrald allowed. He uncoiled the long line from around his waist and fixed a tight knot to the haft, just below the battered steel hammerhead. "Take the loose end of the rope, lad—and hold tight! Here goes. . . ."

The dwarf hurled the weapon with a smooth overhand toss, aiming close to the side of the floor-to-ceiling column of stone. Trailing the rope behind, the hammer whirled through the air, crossed the chasm, and flew into the darkness on the other side. Abruptly it reversed course, flipping back into Fenrald's hand. The rope merely dangled into the chasm, unconnected, for the weapon had not circled the pillar of stone.

Holt shook his head in despair, but Fenrald brightened perceptibly. "This is going to work! Keep a grip on that rope while I try again."

The dwarf threw his weapon in the same fashion, but as soon as it left his hand, he skipped sideways several steps. The hammer and rope flew across the chasm into the shadowy cavern beyond. When the hammer reversed its course, however, it veered to the side in order to return directly to the dwarf. That curve took it around the column of stone, and when the magical weapon had once again returned to Fenrald's hand, he and Holt each held one end of the rope, and the center was looped about the column.

"Good work!" cried the Daryman, straining to keep his voice down.

"That was the easy part," warned Fenrald. "This'll be harder than that bridge crossing— there's nothing to brace your feet on."

Holt was immediately sobered by this knowledge, and by another look into the deep, apparently bottomless chasm. In the depths, impossibly far below, he saw the glow of crimson light, a subterranean fire partially obscured by its own smoke. He could feel the dry heat baking his face, and didn't need a lot of imagination to picture his or Fenrald's fate if either slipped into that abyss.

"I've got a good foothold here for the belay," Fenrald said, squatting on the floor and planting his boots against a solid outcrop of rock. "I'll keep both ends of the rope tied off so you can go hand over hand. D'you think you can get out on the far side?"

Holt studied the place where the rope was wrapped around the stone column. The surface of the rock below seemed rough and broken, so he nodded, hopeful that he would find footholds there.

Suddenly another thought occurred to him.

"How are *you* going to get across?" he asked. "There's no place on this side to tie the rope, and I'll be over there already!"

"I've got me an idea," the dwarf said with a hearty twinkle in his eye. "Let's worry about you, first."

Knowing Fenrald would give no further explanation, Holt sheathed his sword, checked the straps on his backpack, and stepped to the edge of the chasm. The dwarf's solid muscles gave only an inch or two as he leaned his weight on the rope and stretched almost prone above the floor. His cleated boots braced against a stub of rock.

"Ready?" Holt asked.

Fenrald nodded grimly. The Daryman saw the sinews bulging in his friend's arms, sensed the power in that short, muscular body. With a murmur of hope, Holt leaned outward, grasping each of the ropes with one of his hands. For a moment, he swayed sickeningly and feared his weight would prove too much for the dwarf. But Fenrald held firm.

Gradually the lurching motion settled until the Daryman was hanging still, suspended far above the fires in Skyspire's bowels.

Trying to ignore the yawning space beneath his dangling feet, Holt began to inch his way across, sliding his hands—one at a time—along the rough strands of the rope. Laboriously, he advanced, though each tiny movement sent him swinging back and forth. He felt the heat wash over him, rising from below, and could imagine the subterranean fires hungering for him with an appetite as voracious as the dragon's.

Roughly, he forced those thoughts aside, concentrating on the dangerous passage. Halfway across, his palms and fingers began to sting, scraped raw from their passage along the rope. Burning streams of sweat trickled into his eyes, but he didn't dare wipe them away. Each breath was like a taste of fire—hot, dry, and acrid. Nearly blinded, grimacing against the burning pain of blisters and cramps, he strained toward the far side of the chasm.

He kicked his feet, striking the rough rock below the stone pillar and wedging his boot into a narrow crack. Pulling himself forward to where the rope met the pillar, Holt was able to grasp several handholds. Ignoring the bottomless pit gaping behind him, he scrambled around the column, pulled himself over the lip of the precipice, and sprawled, gasping, on the cavern floor.

Wiping the moisture from his forehead and eyes, Holt looked back to see Fenrald's fiercely triumphant grin. The Daryman smiled weakly in return, then dropped his backpack to the floor. He had a suspicion about the dwarf's plan for crossing the chasm, though he hoped he was wrong. Fenrald jabbed the shaft of his hammer firmly through his belt, then seized the two ends of the line. Still grinning, the bearded warrior positioned himself on the lip of the chasm. Holt's fear had been justified. Wrapping the ropes around his wrists several times, Fenrald nodded once, then stepped off the precipice.

The Daryman grimaced in apprehension as the dwarf swung through the air, arcing swiftly downward on the rope. With a resounding *thunk,* Fenrald smashed into the wall forty feet below, bounced away, then swung forward again. Holt grasped at the rope where it came around the pillar, seizing the line and straining to pull upward as he felt his sturdy friend begin to climb.

The hair on the back of Holt's neck bristled. Hissing a warning, he eased the rope back down and urged Fenrald to stay put. At the same time, he flipped open his backpack and snatched out the Crown of Vanderthan.

He felt rather than saw the immense figure of the wyrm advance from the depths of the cavern. Holt placed the crown on his head and crawled toward the wall of the cave, dragging his backpack with him.

Despite his caution, with the crown in place Holt felt no fear. Finding shelter between two shadowy spires of stone, he stared outward, calm and self-assured. He began to think about a way to kill the dragon, pondering several ideas but discarding them all as impractical.

The crown increased his perceptions in the

darkness, and he clearly saw Xtan slinking along the floor. The dragon advanced like a lizard, massive wings tucked, creeping on the mighty tree trunks of his legs. Breathing deeply, with rumbling growls shaking the air, Xtan drew closer.

Holt watched as the monster paused at the chasm, barely a dozen paces away. The Daryman felt a certain appreciation of the dragon's size and power, but experienced none of his earlier fear of the crimson serpent.

One swordlike talon came forward and touched the rope around the pillar.

A tiny voice somewhere deep in Holt's mind reminded him that the dwarf still hung from that line, exposed on the wall of the chasm. It would be a long fall for the hammer-wielder.

The dragon didn't look over the ledge, but a cruel leer twisted his serpentine face as that sharp talon hooked the rope and, with a sharp tug, separated it.

Immediately, both ends of the rope vanished, snapped downward by the weight at the end of the line.

The Daryman felt a sense of vague disappointment—the dwarf had proven useful in the past. Holt's task would be more difficult now that he was alone. Coolly, he watched the dragon spread his wings, soar over the chasm in a single, fluid pounce, and then continue toward the mouth of the lair.

Douglas Niles

As soon as the serpent was out of sight, Holt rose from concealment, shrugged his pack over his shoulders, and—still wearing the Crown of Vanderthan—marched deeper into the darkness.

Princess Danis of Vanderthan, he remembered, was alive somewhere before him. He continued with a firm, steady step, not really sure why this knowledge should be important to him.

18
Cloud of the Crown

Onward went the Daryman, through the descending tunnel of Xtan's lair. Even in places of utter darkness, the Crown of Vanderthan let him see the cavern ceiling sweeping far over his head, the rough and rocky walls rising to either side.

The dwarf had fallen, he remembered, the knowledge causing him a vague sense of unease that he quickly brushed aside. It was right that he advance into this place alone. What other human—what mortal of any kind—could wield the kind of power available to Holton Jaken?

His body tingled with energy, and his mind

twisted and turned along a multitude of pathways.
He knew an overwhelming sense of power and was
propelled by the firm knowledge that his might
should be put to use. The Daryman could wield
that power, he *would* wield it . . . against those who
deserved to be destroyed.

Holt was mildly surprised to realize that his
enemies were not as easy to identify as his memory suggested they should be. The dragon Xtan, of
course, should be killed. In the wyrm's audacious
theft of the woman, his dangerous lust to possess
the crown, the crimson serpent presented a clear
danger. The thought of driving the Lodestone
Blade through the beast's scaly skin appealed to
the Daryman—though, in a moment of crystalline
intuition, he remembered that the dragon was too
large for the sword to reach his heart or any other
vital organ. He searched his imagination, trying to
decide upon an appropriate means of execution.

Perhaps he should use the weapon to cut off the
dragon's head. The notion had definite attraction.
The sinuous neck was no thicker than a man's
trunk—the gray stone blade was certainly long
enough to sever that snakelike extension.

Holt knew that other enemies lurked nearby,
and that he should kill them too. But who were
they? The wererats? The vile lycanthropes were
hardly worthy of his attentions. It would be more
fitting to command them, to mold them into a force
of killing and destruction, an army he could lead

wherever he chose.

A force of Entropy, he realized. The thought sent a shiver through him, but it was not a reaction of fright or revulsion. Instead, the picture caused him an odd thrill of excitement—the first strong emotion he'd felt since donning the crown.

On he walked, one hand resting lightly on the hilt of his sword. He saw no signs of life. The rocks were dry, the floor and walls barren, the air increasingly warm. As he went farther, fiery plumes snaked through cracks in the rocky floor, providing more illumination, and casting shimmering shadows across the soot-covered walls. The power of the crown augmented these dim flares, letting Holt see into deep darkness and glimpse what lay around the next bend of the wide, winding tunnel.

It was this perception that told him he drew close to a woman. After a moment's reflection, he remembered that her name was Danis Vanderthan. She was beautiful, but more importantly, she was *power*. A princess, heir to a proud and longstanding throne—she could be very useful.

Holt resolved to take her.

He came around the bend and saw the human female beside a great monolith of rock. Twin chains linked her wrists to heavy bolts sunk deep into the stone. She sat, looking up at him, and he remembered again that her name was Danis, that she was the First Daughter of Vanderthan. A voice in the dim recesses of his mind suggested that there was much, much more he should be feeling, but that sound was like the yapping of a distant dog—bothersome, but irrelevant. Holt wrestled with a brief sense of annoyance. The Crown of Vanderthan conveyed great wisdom along with its other powers. Why, then, was he so confused?

The expression on the woman's face was strange, distorted by a peculiar wetness falling from her eyes. Her mouth opened and closed, and she made an annoying wail . . . perplexing. She was the reason he had come here, though he still couldn't recall what urgency had driven him. He advanced to her side and—still ignoring the odd noises she made—drew his sword and raised it over his head.

A quick slash chopped the chain holding her right wrist. A second blow cut through the links on her left. Only when he felt her arms around him, dimly sensed the desperation of her embrace, did other memories start to filter through the haze of the crown's power. She was warm, this Danis, and there was an undeniable, if remote, pleasure in the touch of her lips to his face.

A twinge tugged at his awareness, rousing Holt's curiosity. Why should it please him that this woman pressed her mouth to his? The crown . . . it should help him understand! Instead, it seemed now to fog his awareness, to prevent him from knowledge that should otherwise come easily.

He reached to his brow, touching the platinum

circlet. Again he saw the woman, and from some distant place, he heard the unspoken plea in her face and her eyes. But no . . . he had *power* . . . places to go, deeds to accomplish. This human female was a tool that would help him . . . that was all.

Or was it?

She looked at him with an intensity that, even through the cloudy filter of the crown, unsettled him, reminded him of forgotten treasures. Think. Impossible. The Crown of Vanderthan was an iron-clad lock, a barrier against his true being.

With a sudden gesture, Holt snatched the crown off his head, trembling as he held the hateful thing in his hands. A full surge of emotion swept over him, and he groaned in awful dismay. Looking at the princess, he all but choked on his own guilt, pleading for forgiveness. Danis reached for him and pulled him close, burying her face against his chest.

"I knew you'd come," Danis said, sniffling back her tears. "I'm frightened for you—I wish you hadn't! But I knew you would!"

"Of course—I had to! I was terrified when that monster carried you away—"

"Shh," she soothed, again pressing her lips to his.

Pulling her close, Holt felt the princess melting against him, and he wanted to wrap her in a barrier of complete protection.

But there was another awareness within him, something watching . . . pulling.

A glowing eye was examining him, glaring hotly against his scalp—but no! It was the moon, boring even through the thickness of Skyspire . . . another compulsion, wild, dangerous, fierce. Desperately, the Daryman fought against the infernal tugging, the ripples of pain distorting his back. Danis was still in his arms, and he made her the center of his awareness—his sun, his moon, and all his stars.

"It was the crown," he groaned, remembering his aloof detachment when he found her. "It fogged my mind! I didn't know . . . didn't *feel*—"

A new flash of horror rushed through his mind. "By the Spheres—*Fenrald!* He's gone, fallen into the depths—and *I* let him die!"

Guilt choked him. He pulled away from Danis, staring with loathing at the Crown of Vanderthan. It took all of his will not to hurl the thing into the darkest depths of the dragon's lair.

Instead, he turned back to the princess and forced himself to speak through his anguish. "I've got to go back to the chasm—where he fell. There's a chance he's caught on a ledge! He might be alive."

"Yes! Let's go!"

They turned toward the darkened passageway. Despite the shadows, the Daryman gave no thought to donning the crown. Instead, he stuffed it into his backpack, taking the Lodestone Blade in one hand and Danis's hand in the other.

Something flew through the air, sweeping down the center of the vast cavern. It was too small to be the dragon, but Holt raised his sword and stood warily, fearing some new attacker.

The soaring object swept closer, and out of the darkness came the beaming, white-bearded face of Tellist Tizzit. The wizard sat, cross-legged, atop a floating platform—and a healthy-looking Syssal Kipican looked over his shoulder.

"This is the carpet you stretched Syssal on," the wizard explained. "But who would have thought? It flies!"

The magic carpet swept up to the princess and the Daryman, settling gently to the floor. With a creaking of his ancient joints, Tellist rose and tottered forward. "Tut, tut—this damp air is hard on my old bones," he said with a grimace of genuine pain. "But all that aside, you should know that the treasure hoard was really quite a remarkable trove!"

"But—your wounds?" asked Holt as Syssal followed Tellist. The elf walked with his old, supple grace. His eyes were filled with relief at the sight of Danis Vanderthan.

"Potions of healing." The elf clapped Holt on the shoulder. "One of those bottles was enough to cure both of us—Tellist and I each had a drink, and our wounds vanished."

"Quite remarkable, actually," the wizard agreed.

"Fenrald?" Holt asked frantically. "Did you see him?" Again he felt the loathing for the artifact, and the fear of its overwhelming power. Quickly he described the circumstances of his last glimpse of Fenrald.

"Go back to that chasm—fly down and look for him! Please! He might still be alive!"

Remembering the sweeping plunge into smoldering heat, Holt knew it wasn't likely. How could he have left the place without even searching for his friend?

"Please—you've got to try to find him!"

"Of course! Tut, tut—Syssal, you'd best stay here in case he turns up. I don't think the carpet will carry more than two of us."

"Surely—and good luck," the elf said as Tellist mounted his flying rug and rose slowly from the ground. Abruptly the floating platform spun about, the wizard raising a cautionary finger. "Tut, tut—I'm getting absentminded in my old age. I forgot to tell you the *really* important news!"

"Is it about the dragon, or the crown?" Danis blurted.

"Both, actually. You see, the way to destroy the crown *does* involve fire, and—just as Whisktale told us—we'll find it in the Wyrmrange. But it's not just throwing it into a fiery hole in the ground as we first thought!"

"What *is* it?" Holt demanded.

"Why, dragon's breath, surprisingly enough."

"How do you know that?"

"Remarkable thing—a crystal ball, I guess you'd call it. It was in the treasure room, sitting in a niche in the wall. While we waited there, this image came into the glass sphere—a knight, with a full-face visor, with a message for Xtan.

"I was able to work a little illusion—nothing spectacular, just made myself look like a fire-breathing, man-eating red dragon—weighing about thirteen tons, give or take a few thousand pounds. The resemblance must have worked, because this knight mistook me for our serpentine friend. He lifted his visor and started to speak." The wizard shuddered visibly at the memory.

"Tut, tut—I don't mind telling you that his appearance was not something you'd want a young child to see—or a grown man, for that matter. Face was half rotted away, just these glowing spots for eyes. He was an altogether—"

"What did he *say*?" Holt urged.

"My point, precisely. He told Xtan—that is, *me*—that somebody . . . 'Dallipher' or some such . . . had told him how the crown could be destroyed. He warned me—that is, Xtan—to be careful not to breath on the crown. It's dragonfire—the burning kind, not my horse—that will destroy the artifact and thus solve all our problems rather neatly, don't you think?"

"But the dragon breathed on me when I wore the crown," Danis argued. "The artifact wasn't affected *then*."

"Ah—because you were *wearing* it!" the mage pointed out. "When you wear the crown, you and everything you're holding or wearing is invulnerable! But if you take the crown off, that invulnerability is not in effect. *Then,* if the dragon breathes on you, the crown will be destroyed!"

"But so will whoever's holding it," Holt objected, horrified.

"What? Er, I think you're right. Tut, tut—it seems I hadn't fully considered that. I'm afraid that would be the case, though . . . and it's a problem, to be sure."

"No more time to talk about it," Holt said grimly, feeling the hackles rising on his neck. He pointed up the tunnel of the dragon's lair.

They all felt the ominous evil of the monster's presence even before the crimson form swept into view. A rush of air roared down the cavern, pressing against their ears, heavy with menace and decay.

"Quickly! Hide!" cried the princess, pulling Holt behind the pillar of rock where she had been imprisoned.

Tellist and Syssal leapt onto the speeding carpet and flew for the shadows on the far side of the cavern.

"Come on—down here!" Holt urged Danis, seeing a narrow crack between the pillars at the near edge of the cave. He pushed her inside, then followed,

reaching into his pack to once again take the crown
in hand. Squatting below the level of sight, he
turned and cautiously raised his eyes.

When he peered over the rocks, he saw crimson
wings and the unblinking spots of leering, vicious
eyes. Those golden ovals probed the darkness,
seeking with murderous intent.

Xtan had returned.

19
The Heart of Skyspire

"Let's go!" Holt hissed, putting his hand on Danis's shoulder and gently urging her down the tunnel, deeper into the cave.

The dragon was a palpable presence behind them, swelling from the utter darkness, surging forward as relentlessly as an incoming tide.

"But—the crown!" she demurred. "We've got to get Xtan to breathe on it!"

"Do you think we should *ask* him?" Holt whispered in exasperation. "Let's get to somewhere safer for now—*then* we can make some kind of plan!"

Despite her reluctance, Danis allowed the Daryman to push her along. Holt looked backward once, seeing no sign of the elf and wizard on their flying carpet—he could only hope they had reached a safe hiding place.

The man and woman clung to the shadows near the wall of the tunnel, slipping from rock to rock as they felt the ominous rush of the dragon's approach. The pair scuttled through a narrow side cavern linked through many openings to the main passage of the dragon's lair. Holt looked back again and saw the eerie glow of one of Xtan's huge eyes before the two of them ducked around a corner.

Even as they skidded away, Holt felt a flash of hope. The crown *could* be destroyed! He only had to figure out a way to accomplish that task without exposing Danis to fatal danger.

The Daryman lunged after the princess, tripped, and flopped onto the floor with a clatter of stones. His limbs seemed to move through syrup, struggling against the commands of his brain—why was he suddenly so *clumsy?* Holt clawed at rough handholds, trying to pull himself upward—and then one of his hands came down on the back of the other, and he froze.

Stiff, unnatural hair bristled from his skin. He could see it sprouting against his palm, growing even now. He *saw* it grow despite the utter darkness! Biting back a groan of horror, he touched his face, feeling the rippling of his skin as his body began to change. A choking, strangled gasp forced its way from his mouth as Holt twisted, bending double. Cramps racked his torso, and he retched violently, falling to the ground.

"Holt?" The princess, her whispered voice raw with concern, knelt beside him. Holt feared she would touch him, feel the unnatural transformation of his skin and body. "What happened? Are you hurt?"

"Danis . . ." He recoiled, knowing he had to stop her. In a flash, the truth came to him, and somehow he forced his distorted mouth to form the words.

"I love you!" he gasped, reaching for her hand.

Finding it, his fingers were once again normal human digits. Choking back the unseen call of the moon, he willed the transformation to cease. After a moment, he felt his strength return, and gasping for breath, he scrambled to his feet and continued on.

From behind came a rumble of heavy breath— an exhalation of rage as Xtan found the broken chains and saw that his captive was missing.

Not pausing to look back, Holt and the princess sprinted through the shadows, following the gradual descent of the corridor as they curved away from the lair. The Daryman tucked the crown under a flap of his wool vest, masking the illumination from the dragon's eyes. Flames brightened these caverns in fiery light, pulses of orange that flashed from around the winding corners or rose through deep cracks in the floor. All of these, Holt saw with relief, were the irregular flickers of subterranean heat, not the scalding inferno of the dragon's breath.

"Here!" Danis whispered, pulling against the Daryman's hand to halt him in place. She indicated a narrow, dark cut in the side of the cave. "It's too small for him to follow us!"

"All right," Holt agreed. "You go first."

She nodded and ducked into the narrow aperture, which was too tight for the two of them to proceed side by side. Holt held the Crown of Vanderthan against his belly, shielding the glow of the artifact with his body. If the dragon followed them and belched his fiery breath, he would toss the artifact into the cloud—and shield the princess with his own flesh, if it came to that.

Abruptly Danis yelped and dropped away. Holt grabbed for her, tumbling forward as his feet skidded off a steep, unseen lip. He clawed frantically at the graveled slope beneath him, terrified he would crash into the princess and hurt her. Abruptly he heard a thud and rolled to the side, jarring to a stop against a looming boulder.

"Are you all right?" Danis asked.

He whispered an affirmative.

They had tumbled into a region of utter darkness, but the Daryman heard her sit up and dust herself off beside him.

Holt drew a ragged breath, startled as his respiration became a snarl—an *animal's* growl! He felt a gnawing hunger, more acute than any emptiness he had ever felt. For a moment, all he could think about was flesh, warm blood . . . *feeding*. Grimacing, he felt his own sharp teeth prodding his lips, distorting the shape of his jaws.

"No!" he groaned, leaning backward hard enough to smash his skull against the cavern wall.

Danis! His thoughts turned to her, and the image of her golden hair, the warmth of her smile, gave him an anchor against the chaos that racked him. Shaken, he clenched his fists, willing himself not to change. Sweat beaded on his forehead, but when he wiped it away, he felt weak with relief—his hand was a human's, again.

"Holt—what is it?" Danis spoke to him from the darkness.

He focused on her voice, her presence. Reaching out for her, he wrapped his fingers in hers and squeezed.

"I—I'm all right," he said. "Just glad I found you, that's all." He hoped he was telling the truth—even as he recognized the lie.

Slowly Holt lifted the artifact from his lap, where he had masked the crown's illumination with the flap of his tunic. Danis stared at him, wide-eyed, concerned—but not the slightest bit afraid. The Daryman tried to quell his own tremors of fear, raising the circlet over his head so that they could get a look at their surroundings.

They had fallen into a large, circular grotto, with walls scoured by ancient, infernal fires. In many places, the walls were creased by narrow cracks and loose rubble. Several small niches showed as darker shadows in the walls, while the mouth of a large cavern loomed across the chamber.

Danis sat beside the Daryman, and for long, timeless moments, they rested in bleak silence. Holt set the Crown of Vanderthan on the floor. The artifact shed its gentle, pearly light, and the glow made fireflies in Danis's golden hair. Holt reached out, touched those silken tresses, pulled her close.

"I feel like we're in the foundations of the world," the princess said finally, with a sigh that came perilously close to hopelessness. "What can we do?"

"We'll find a way out of here," Holt pledged, squeezing her hand in his.

"Whatever happens . . . we'll be together, won't we?"

"Yes—we . . . we *have* to be!"

"I never could have married anyone else," the princess said suddenly, slipping her other hand into both of his. "I don't care *what* my father would have said—he couldn't make me take a husband I didn't want!"

Holt sighed, warmed by her statement. "He wasn't about to let *me* have you," he pointed out.

"I don't care!" Danis said fiercely. "I would have been an old maid, then!"

The Daryman wrapped his aching arms around her. "What about the realm? Vanderthan needs a king, doesn't it?"

"I don't see why I couldn't just be a queen, all by myself!" she retorted.

"I can't hold you from your destiny, and I won't stand in the way of your life!" he assured, each word true—and each adding to the pain in his heart.

"Your life and mine belong together! *I* can see that, even if my father can't!"

Holt tried to speak, but again his thoughts seemed cloudy, vague. Cramps writhed along the muscles of his arms, shoulders, and back, and he flinched involuntarily, uttering a deep, bestial grunt.

"Holt! You're—changing!" Danis pulled back, her eyes wide and, in the pale light of the crown, luminous. Yet she was not afraid, at least not for herself; she reached out a soothing hand to take his twisting forearm.

"No!" he denied, horrified as the word came out in a desperate snarl. Already his humanity was fading. He sensed that the woman was weak, vulnerable. Hunger began to gnaw at him with a force that couldn't be denied. Her identity faded, and she became something basic, appealing only to his most primitive need . . . she was *prey!*

Stones clattered beside them, and Danis stifled a scream, looking past Holt's shoulder.

The Daryman whirled, his lip curling into an involuntary snarl as a shape lunged from the darkness. He saw a bristling snout framing glaring yellow fangs, and shook his head in disbelief— was he looking at a mirror image of himself?

The dark form leapt closer, and red eyes flashed greedily. Two clawed hands reached out with snakelike quickness, snatching the artifact from the stone floor. Hissing with instinctive hatred, the Daryman recognized the pointed nose, the wicked, twisted sneer of triumph.

"Whisktale!" Danis spat furiously. The princess reached for the Crown of Vanderthan, but the wererat slashed her hand aside. Wrapping black talons around the circlet of metal, the vile creature whirled to leap away.

"My master shall have it!" sneered the grotesque monster that had been the seer of Rochester. The bristling back vanished into the darkness, accompanied by a clatter of rocks as the beast bounded up a steep shelf of rock. A lingering stench in the air stung Holt's keen nostrils, filling him with unquenchable rage.

The Daryman sprang after the wererat, possessed by pure, murderous instinct. He threw himself at the wall and clawed upward. Grasping tiny knobs of rock, he bounded ten feet higher, then pounced again and again, climbing in a way no human ever could. More importantly, he drew closer to Whisktale with each upward leap.

Holt's vision cleared, and he saw the giant rat springing before him, the crown clutched in its mouth. Whisktale reached a high ledge and spun, crouching on all fours, facing Holt with bared fangs.

The crown clattered to the stones, resting against the cliff wall as the Daryman flung himself at his enemy's throat. Snarls and growls echoed through the cavern, the cries of the two lycanthropes forming a horrid chorus.

Holt's fangs ripped into flesh. Whisktale shrieked in pain, twisting to bite the transformed Daryman in the shoulder. The two creatures, both now covered in bristling fur, clenched each other with claws, biting and snarling. Tails lashed across the narrow ledge, and the crown went flying, clattering down the cliff.

Poised at the lip of the ledge, Holt twisted desperately. He raked Whisktale's sides with his talons. Then the two were falling, smashing off rocks, bouncing down the cliff. Still the Daryman kept his hold on the grotesque body that squirmed beneath his paws. Whisktale shrieked and twisted frantically, but Holt sought his enemy's throat with crushing jaws and held the craven seer below him. The two beasts smashed to the ground at the foot of the cliff, but still they remained clenched, rolling and tumbling across the floor.

In a powerful bite, the Daryman's fangs tore through the stiff fur of his foe's pulsing throat. With a final shudder, the wererat died. Holt raised his head, glaring wildly, trembling with triumph and fury. He growled as he felt the body below him shifting. The monstrous corpse twisted and distorted until it was human, recognizable as the man who had served Gallarath so treacherously.

"Holt? Holt . . . it's me . . . Danis."

He looked at her through bloodshot eyes. The haze of battle lingered, and for a moment, he trembled with an urge to attack.

"Here—the crown. Wear it!" she urged, holding the artifact forward in both hands.

Snatching the circlet from her with animalistic greed, he pulled it to his chest, uncertain what to do.

"Put it *on!*" she urged, desperation tightening her voice.

Something reached him through the fog of hate and fear. Looking at the clawed, furry paws that held the crown, Holt sensed that something was *wrong*. He placed the crown on his brow and pulled back, shuddering under a renewed onslaught of physical transformation. Gagging, he lurched backward, as the power of the potent artifact battled with the curse of Entropy that possessed him.

Then his hands were hands again, his body

whole—

And, once again, his emotions were numbed. He didn't hear the words Danis said as she threw her arms around him, as she sobbed against his chest. Firmly, he pushed her away and stood, looking up the cavern, trying to sense dangers . . . and opportunities.

The dragon was a distant menace, not an immediate threat. Holt looked around, wondering if he could retrace the route he and Danis had followed down here. He was aware of movement before him, and his keen eyes penetrated the darkness with ease.

"They come," he said.

"Tut, tut—how's that?"

Holt heard the words, and in another moment, a wash of light flowed through the narrow confines of the cavern.

"Tellist! Down here!" cried Danis, looking upward.

The glow of the light spell revealed the wizard, as well as Syssal Kipican and Fenrald Falwhak, peering down at them. The three companions leaned over the lip of a ledge, perhaps thirty feet over their heads.

"Fenrald!" The princess's voice was a gasp of delight as the bearded face above broke into a broad grin.

"The dwarf is alive," Holt remarked, vaguely pleased by the discovery.

"Here—let me throw you the rope!" Fenrald said. In moments, the line snaked down to them, and they scrambled out of the deep pit.

"How—what happened?" stammered Danis, clasping the sputtering dwarf in a bear hug.

"Well, I landed on a pretty wide ledge right after the dragon cut the rope. Thought I'd be stuck there forever till good old Tellist came along with his flying carpet! We even managed to save the rope!"

"And it's a good thing," she declared, blinking back tears of relief.

"We're wasting time . . . I must kill the dragon," Holt declared.

"No!" Danis objected in panic—but the emotion was a distant blur to the Daryman.

He rose to his feet and started walking, ignoring the murmured conversation of the companions behind him. Remembering the lycanthropy that had earlier seized him, Holt knew that the power of the crown held the curse in check. If he removed the artifact, no doubt he would once again be transformed—but there was no danger of that. He would keep the artifact on his head, perhaps for the rest of his life.

"We'd better get moving," Fenrald said gruffly. "That wyrm is still squirming around in here. I get the feeling he'd like to find us!"

Abruptly a looming shape rose in the cavern before them, and the ominous growl of the dragon's breathing rumbling through the air.

"I see that you have brought my artifact," the red dragon sneered, fastening his yellow eyes on the crown resting firmly on Holt's head. Raising his sinuous neck, Xtan gazed down from far above them, then leaned forward as if he might strike at any moment.

"Well—if it isn't that big lizard," Fenrald declared with a snort. "How come you're not off playing with the rest of the snakes?"

"Amusing bravado," chuckled the monster. "Quite appropriate for one's last words, I should think."

Holt was barely listening. Instead, he looked around the cavern, seeking some means to slay the dragon. He saw a number of small, dark holes around the periphery of the large chamber, but Xtan could reach any one of them with a simple pounce. Even if the monster could barely fit his head inside the smaller of the niches, the other companions would not be able to flee far enough to escape the incinerating furnace of his breath. Of course, Holt could survive by himself, but he knew that these others could be useful to him. . . .

"Here!" Fenrald whispered, gesturing to a narrow alcove behind them. Holt saw a tunnel no more than four feet in diameter.

"Go! In there!" declared the Daryman. "I will fight the dragon!"

Eyeing his opponent while his companions dived for shelter, Holt realized that the cavern was a bad place to fight—it was large enough for the dragon to use all of his size and power. With that thought, the Daryman turned and ran for a small gap in the tunnel—an opening not so constricting as the one sheltering the companions. Roaring in surprise, the serpent pounced after him.

Holt skidded through the narrow aperture, slid down a steep chute, and tumbled through an entrance to suddenly find himself outside, once again under that shroud of overcast clouds. A high ridge ringed him completely, and plumes of fire burst from the ground nearby.

Abruptly he understood: he stood upon the splintered, rocky surface of Skyspire's crater.

A clatter of stones drew his attention. The huge form of the red dragon flowed from the cliff nearby, emerging from a wider tunnel near the one Holt had used. The wyrm rushed toward the man, and blocked any escape.

Holt drew the Lodestone Blade. With the crown on his head and the gray stone sword in his hand, he was ready to meet the dragon.

20
Duel for a Crown

Xtan reared back in surprise, and the mighty jaws gaped, ready for a flaming exhalation. No matter, thought Holt—the crown was placed firmly on the Daryman's head, and its power would protect both the man and the artifact itself. But at the last minute the wyrm clamped his jaws shut and reached a taloned forepaw for the human. Perhaps Xtan wished to save his fiery cloud for a more vulnerable target.

Holt stabbed, the blade clashing into a hard claw, then slicing through scales to draw a shriek of inhuman pain from the rearing monstrosity.

Xtan writhed upward, and in the next instant, the Daryman darted past, racing across the floor of the crater.

"You shall *die,* human!" bellowed the dragon, pouncing after him, shaking the ground with the force of his landing.

The splintered rocks of the crater floor jutted upward like surreal tree trunks, a forest scorched by an unspeakable blaze. Holt skirted a pair of these outcrops, then skidded along the lip of a deep crevasse as fire belched upward. Tendrils of flame stroked his legs, his chest, and face, until his boots smoked and his tunic was scorched by the heat. But the crown's immunity protected his skin, and he felt no more than a steady warmth, which dissipated as he darted away from the chasm, dodging around more looming hummocks of rock.

One of these looked like a human head, a gargantuan face leering at him in the light of nearby blazes. Another seemed to mimic the form of a hunched bear, impossibly monstrous, glowering and looming murderously. But these were just rocks, twisted and distorted by heat and pressure perhaps, but useful only as obstacles to the dragon and concealment for the human. Holt crouched behind one of these, then darted to another as the serpent approached.

Xtan leapt again, but Holt turned to meet the attack with a slash of his blade, forcing the serpent's head back, out of range. Again those jaws gaped, and again the dragon restrained his infernal breath.

Holt remembered his earlier intention with sudden amazement—he had momentarily considered *voluntarily* offering the artifact for destruction! No more.

He climbed away from the wyrm, moving up the sloping floor, stabbing the Lodestone Blade between the flaring nostrils when Xtan snapped at him. A mighty claw bashed the man to the side, dull pain rising in his shoulder. Yet that obscure ache was a distant agony, something that one as mighty as the Daryman could merely shrug away.

Now he skirted a deep crevasse, glancing downward at a stream of lava bubbling a thousand feet below. Flames billowed high and bright in a sudden, surging geyser, bright light briefly outlining his shadow on the wall of the crater. The image of himself, a hundred feet high, was vaguely pleasing to the Daryman.

He circled around, back to the cave leading into the mountainside. His companions were there, peering from the shadowy entrance, beckoning, but he had no time for them now.

"Run!" cried the golden-haired woman, the princess, frantically waving him toward the hole.

Xtan's bellows grew shrill, and the wyrm pounced onto Holt, crushing him to the ground. As he fell, the man sliced into a forepaw with that deadly blade, then drove back the killing jaws with an upward stab. He twisted in a grip that would have crushed any normal man, but, slashing back against the dragon's other leg, Holt managed to kick free. Scrambling to his feet, attacking recklessly, he sensed a growing advantage as Xtan retreated from the lethal, bloody blade.

Again he looked at that supple neck and thought: there is my enemy's weakness. But it seemed the dragon, too, sensed the danger. He held his head aloft, lifting the crimson throat beyond the reach of the deadly blade while driving at the Daryman with taloned forepaws.

Red scales flashed from the darkness as Xtan suddenly brought his tail around, slamming it into Holt. Gasping, the man stumbled to the side. He clutched his sword in a determined effort not to lose his weapon. The Daryman fell heavily, tumbling over the rocky ground, clawing with his free hand to stop his slide at the lip of a fiery chasm. Precariously balanced, nearly slipping, Holt struggled for purchase—still keeping a tight grip on his treasured sword.

He kicked to his knees and then, slowly, scrambled to his feet as the wyrm crept forward like a cat stalking a mouse. Though the crown remained on Holt's head, his mind was foggy, clouded by the force of the blow. The crimson serpent faded in and out of sight.

Knowing that in his grogginess he was vulnerable, Holt darted around a nearby pillar of stone, slid into a shallow depression, and crawled past

another screening ridge of rock. He halted near the cave that concealed the others, and crouched out of sight of the dragon.

A cascade of white whiskers materialized nearby as Tellist Tizzit suddenly tottered into view, mumbling to himself, stumbling around an outcrop of rock. He stood over the Daryman, offering a hand. "Tut, tut—Holton, my boy. Stand up—that's no way to win a fight!"

The serpent crept closer as Holt stumbled up to the ancient wizard. "Take shelter!" the young swordsman ordered. "I cannot offer you safety."

"Well, of course—er, but perhaps I could stand behind you?" suggested Tellist amiably.

The Daryman stepped forward, already forgetting the mage—until he felt the old man's hand at the back of his head. Holt reached back, rage swelling at the betrayal, and he felt Tellist's fingers wrapping around the tines of the gem-studded circlet.

The wizard snapped a single word, and he disappeared—and with him went the Crown of Vanderthan.

"No!"

Shocked, the Daryman bellowed a cry of fury, anguish, and fear—the full flood of emotions that had been masked by the artifact. He spun, seeking the wizard, knowing Tellist Tizzit had teleported somewhere.

Yet already his initial outrage was tempered by

confusion ... *why* had the wizard taken the crown? He wasn't the Daryman's enemy. Or was he? With an instinctive growl, Holt curled around, unnatural hunger once again aching in his belly.

Fenrald dived out from concealment behind a rock, tackling Holt—and then Syssal was there too, seizing the struggling man by the forearms. His two friends dragged him through the narrow mouth of the cavern as the Daryman growled and flailed.

The moon again called to him, compelled his body to change, his will to surrender to the curse of Entropy.

Words came from the crater and, dimly, Holt heard the wizard speaking; the Daryman ceased his struggles and turned bright hysterical eyes toward the mage.

"Tut, tut, beast—are you as full of hot air as has been rumored?"

"No!" screamed Danis from the cave mouth, watching in horror as Tellist appeared on the far side of Xtan.

"Arrogant, insolent fool! You will *die!*" bellowed Xtan.

The wizard's hands were clutched behind his back, and he laughed curtly in the enraged serpent's face.

The Daryman broke away from the elf and dwarf, scrambling to his feet. Without the crown shoring up his will, he felt the growing compulsion of the full moon glowing evilly above the clouds. The summons of Entropy was strong, almost irresistible, but when he saw the courageous mage standing before the looming horror of the red dragon, he strived to hold the transformation at bay.

Tellist looked surprisingly frail, like a very old man, as he stood before the serpent, grinning foolishly into the monster's glowering eyes. And then Holt saw—it *wasn't* foolishness! In the wizard's eyes, grim and purposeful, gleamed a light of utter courage.

Xtan's jaws gaped, and a billowing cloud of fire erupted, surrounding the wizard and the crown. There was no sound but the furious roar of those flames, burning, greedily consuming, raging in a torrent of unspeakable power—and horrific, destructive heat. Crackling into an oily, spuming cloud, the inferno belched smoke and radiated pure heat.

Sobbing, the princess turned her eyes away while Holt, gawking in horror, watched the fireball recede. Only blackened ashes remained. Not even the Crown of Vanderthan had survived, and it was this realization that drove Xtan to a bellow of fury.

The artifact was gone.

Holt trembled, grieving for Tellist—and fighting the compulsion that, once again, ripped through his body. He felt the claws struggling to tear through his fingertips, and moaned insensately as

he clenched his hands into fists, striving to reverse
the corruption.

Shrilly braying, the dragon whirled on the sur-
viving companions and lunged toward the narrow
tunnel mouth. His fiery breath could quickly
engulf and kill them all.

Danis—he had to find a way to protect her!

"Holt! Let's go! *Run!*" The princess tugged at
him while Syssal and Fenrald started farther into
the narrow cave. The Daryman stumbled against
the wall, forcing himself to stand upright.

Though the entrance to the passage was very
narrow, he saw that it expanded to a high ceiling
within. On the inside of the doorway was a ledge,
and on an impulse of hope, Holt leapt upward,
scrambling to a perch just above—and inside—the
narrow tunnel mouth. Somehow his hand
remained clenched around the hilt of his sword.

"Go!" he hissed at Danis, not certain if the voice
was his own or the wererat's. Everything was
foggy, confused; he growled, hating himself, hating
the changes that racked him, and beginning to feel
that awful, mindless hunger again.

"Run!" snarled the Daryman through clenched
teeth—or fangs. "And no matter what happens—
don't come back!"

"No!" she sobbed, reaching for him.

His lips curled, and an inhuman snarl tore
through the cave. Still crying, Danis hesitated a
moment, until Syssal took her arm and tugged

firmly. Finally, she turned and fled.

Holt balanced precariously over the mouth of the tunnel. If Xtan remained outside, the serpent could spit a fireball through that entrance, and they would all perish.

Trembling seized him with the force of an earthquake, threatening to topple him from his perch. A fog of rage and hate closed in, and if Danis had been close enough he might have attacked her, a nightmare onslaught of fangs, talons . . . and disease. But from a dim recess, his old self spoke, telling him that he was *glad* she was gone.

Then all other thoughts were forgotten as Xtan's broad head bulled through the narrow entrance, jaws gaping wide as Danis, Syssal, and Fenrald disappeared around a bend in the narrow corridor. The dragon's dry, explosive laugh was a bark of cruelty. The monster inhaled, ready to incinerate them all.

The Daryman of Oxvale struck. Holt chopped downward with the Lodestone Blade, striking at the neck exposed so vulnerably below him. He toppled from the ledge, diving, slashing with the weapon. The gray stone blade sliced through crimson scales, and with a dull thunk, the dragon's head toppled free.

There was no fire, no sound other than the thud of lifeless flesh and bone on the rocky floor. With a shuddering convulsion, the headless body jerked backward, clearing the entrance of the cave—then falling still.

Shaking from tension and delayed fear, Holt slipped from the ledge, next to his gory trophy. He raced outside, threw back his head, and howled, his victory cry a bray of Entropy, rising from the floor of the crater, echoing from the mountainous walls, wailing outward toward the moon itself.

White light leaked through the chinks in the overcast. Abruptly the clouds broke, the moon shining down, illuminating the crater. The Lodestone Blade fell from the Daryman's hand—paw, now. He hunched onto all fours, snapped and barked at the sky, arched his ridged, bristling back. He growled loudly, aware of nothing so much as the compelling lure of that circular object.

A winged shape glided past the moon and circled through hot drafts as it settled into the crater. Holt crouched, motionless, watching as a barrel-bodied owl came to rest on the ridged back of the slain dragon.

"I say! This is perhaps the largest corpse I've ever seen!"

Straining to maintain his silence, the wererat that had been a Daryman looked upward, eyeing the creature. Craftily, Holt crouched, silent. If he was patient, the bird would come close enough for the kill.

Abruptly, he was hit from behind. Fenrald and Syssal tackled him, bearing him to the ground. Furiously he struggled. The owl fluttered over, coming to rest on a nearby outcrop of rock. Holt shrieked and snarled, howling like a mad dog—or worse.

"Sir Ira!" Danis cried. "Can you help him?"

The owl hopped to the ground beside Holt, who still growled and snapped, trying to free his taloned paws from the grip of his friends. Holding firm, the elf and the dwarf pinned the Daryman.

Blindly Holt flailed, but he couldn't strike, couldn't *move*. A shimmer of brilliant yellow appeared above him—Danis's hair glowing in the moonlight. The beauty of those golden strands awed him, and his struggles settled as she bent over him, moisture shining from her eyes.

"I think the man needs a curse removed! And I'm just the owl for the job!" Sir Ira remarked. He hopped over to the suddenly serene wererat, extending a broad wing.

The brown feathers trailed across Holt's face, and abruptly the Daryman relaxed. He felt the power of Sir Ira's healing magic seeping through his skin, soaking into flesh and bone, driving the blight of disease from his body. Claws receded from his fingertips, and the aching hunger faded. An aura of warmth and peace spread slowly through his limbs.

Moments later, he slept.

When he awakened it was still night, and he still lay on the sooty ground of the mountain. The moon had moved some distance across the sky, but it no longer drew him with any compulsion other than its serene beauty.

Nearby Holt saw a large horse and blinked, wondering if his eyes deceived him. When the animal turned, however, he saw the torso, the strapping arms and manly head, and he recognized the centaur Gallut. "Where? . . . how? . . ." he stammered in confusion.

A smooth-faced dwarf stepped closer. Felicia, standing with Fenrald's arm locked in hers.

Shaking his head, certain he had lost his senses, the Daryman sat up and touched his face—it felt normal and smooth, with just the budding stubble of his natural beard beginning to layer his chin.

Sir Ira perched on a nearby outcrop of rock, preening his feathers. He puffed out his chest when he saw that Holt was awake, and cleared his throat dramatically.

"Splendid to see you, my good man. You should know that Felicia came to Riftvale several days ago and told me you had been bitten by one of these rotters. She guessed the lot of you were heading for Skyspire, so of course we made haste to come after you."

The owl bowed and, with a flourish of his wing, indicated the centaur. "Indeed, my strong right arm—that is, Gallut, carried her swiftly through the mountains while I flew overhead, trying to find you. It seems we were barely in time."

Sir Ira blinked, and Holt saw the wetness in his

eyes. "In time for you, if not for Tellist. . . ."

The wizard's sacrifice, and the horror of his own transformation, swelled Holt's own throat, and he turned away in shame and grief. Danis knelt beside him, and he lost himself in the warmth of her arms, their tears mingling as the mountainous crater rumbled and flamed all around.

21
Endings and Beginnings

"He gave his life in the highest tradition of noble sacrifice," King Dathwell proclaimed, a catch in his voice halting his words. "Tellist Tizzit died as a hero of the realm, and as such shall he always be remembered."

Beside Holt at the grand table of Castle Vanderthan's feast hall, Fenrald Falwhak loudly blew his nose, while Syssal Kipican looked on in somber grief. Danis turned and buried her face against Holt's shoulder, and the Daryman tried to hold back his own tears as he allowed her to sob out her sorrow.

Gazzrick Whiptoe, seated on the other side of
the king, reached around the monarch to offer a
handkerchief to the distraught princess. Nodding
his thanks, Holt took the cloth. The brave halfling,
at least, had made a full recovery from the murderous attack of the vampire.

Many a tear was blinked back by the assembled
folk of Vanderthan and the surrounding communi-
ties. Tellist Tizzit had been known to many, and
when King Dathwell proclaimed this day of mourn-
ing, the entire population turned out to grieve for
the fallen wizard—and to celebrate the safe return
of the princess and her heroic companions.

Holt saw Felicia sitting beside Fenrald, remembering the dwarf woman's joy when her father had
appointed her official ambassador from Pumice to
Graywall. Fenrald Falwhak, too, had been pleased
by the news, though the dwarf, too, had made the
long journey back to Vanderthan under the oppressive cloud of loss.

The Daryman's mind drifted over the long
weeks of travel. The spring had blossomed into a
full, hot summer, and verdant greenery had
adorned the trees of Karawenn's forests when the
adventurers emerged from the Wyrmrange.

Throughout the long journey, Holt and Danis
had avoided speaking of the future. Instead they
had conversed almost desperately about their surroundings, their nightly camps, the landmarks

they passed. The burdens of royalty had never weighed so heavily on the First Daughter, and—despite his own sense of loss—Holt had been unwilling to add to those burdens. Yet in the depths of his heart he had settled on a hard truth. Soon he would have to tell her.

It would come as no surprise for the princess to learn that he loved her—surely she already knew this! The Daryman even felt certain his desperate affection was returned. It was bitter medicine that the matter of birth and rank stood between them—but King Dathwell remained adamant. Danis would marry a nobleman, someone of station worthy to inherit the throne of Vanderthan.

Holt had realized during those long weeks that he could not live in the same realm as Princess Danis—not when he would have to see her wed to someone else, or know she rejected suitors because of him.

He looked across the crowded great hall to the table where the farmers of Oxvale ate, drank, and celebrated. Derek, Nowell the Aching, Hag Biddlesome, Karl Fisher, and all the others feasted there—neighbors all his life, equals and friends.

Holt was one of them. A Daryman, proud of his heritage, cherishing his freedom. Oxvale was a beautiful place, offering a pastoral setting such as he had found rarely in his travels across Karawenn. In another life, he would have been content to work there, to live out his days tending his herd, selling his cheese in the bustling markets of Vanderthan.

Yet how could he go back now, after all that had happened? Without conscious thought, Holt knew that, just as he couldn't stay in Vanderton, neither could he return to Oxvale—his ancestral home was no longer a place he could live. At this point he didn't know where he would go, but already the urge to be away was growing. Tomorrow, he promised himself, he would mount Old Thunder, pass through the castle gates, and turn his back on the realm forever.

Lost in self-pity, Holt realized only gradually that the attention of all the celebrators had focused on him. The king was saying something, and the young Daryman blinked, forcing himself to pay attention.

". . . regret that it does not lie within my power to alter certain facts—facts of birth, and of life and station. However, as king, I can bestow the great honor of the title: Knight of the Realm."

The applause, punctuated by hearty cheers from the farmers of Oxvale, washed over Holt, but could not penetrate the bleak shroud of his mood.

"Stand up!" Fenrald whispered, digging an elbow into the Daryman's ribs.

Numbly, Holt rose. King Dathwell beamed at him, beckoned him to stand before the royal seat.

"Holton Jaken, in honor of your many accomplishments—and of the selfless aid you have given to the First Daughter—I pronounce you Sir Holton, Knight of Vanderthan!"

The cheers rose to a crescendo, and somehow Holt found the will to kneel. He was vaguely aware of the king's silver blade touching each of his shoulders, but even the pride shining from Danis's eyes barely touched him.

Selfless aid, the king had said! The words struck a bitter chord of irony in Holt's heart, for he knew that his efforts had been far less noble than Dathwell supposed. *All the while I loved her,* the Daryman wanted to shout. *It was not selfless—I wanted her to love me too!*

Danis came to him as he rose, but when she took both of his hands he wanted to pull away. He couldn't draw back, and when she leaned forward to kiss him he returned her embrace with all his strength. His lips met hers, and for a few precious seconds time ceased to move.

"Ahem," the king interjected, with the suggestion of a frown. "I understand your gratitude, my dear—and of course, if there *were* anything I could do. . . ."

"Father, I *will* marry him!"

The silence following the First Daughter's pronouncement was sudden and all-encompassing.

"I love Holton Jaken!" she declared. "And I shall never love another."

Dathwell's frown deepened, and it was as if all the occupants of the great hall held their collective breath, waiting for the royal explosion.

Instead, the monarch sighed, and Holt heard genuine regret in his voice. "Now, my dear, I know the restrictions on your suitors have been an annoyance to you. Perhaps the customs seem frivolous, simple nuisances. I don't think you quite understand the hundreds of years of tradition, the customs—not merely of Vanderthan, but of all Karawenn—that will insure that a worthy husband shall—"

"Worthy?" The scorn in his daughter's voice brought the king's words to an abrupt halt, though a red flush began to creep upward from his straw-colored beard, spreading hotly across his cheeks and forehead.

"There is no man in all Karawenn—in all the Spheres!—who could be more worthy than Holton Jaken! How many times did he risk his life for me, and for your kingdom? He saved me from death, and all the while behaved with honor that most high-born princelings would do well to emulate!"

"Nevertheless—!" The king struggled to interrupt, glowering angrily at his daughter.

"Sire—perhaps there is a solution that has not yet been considered."

The voice came from the table of Oxvale farmers, and Dathwell turned his displeasure toward the speaker. Holt realized that his father had rolled his chair forward, and now boldly faced the king.

"Well, speak up, then!" snapped Dathwell. He crossed his arms and glared at the elder Daryman, at the princess, and at the young man he had just knighted.

"As is well known in Vanderthan, we Darymen of Oxvale and the rest of the emancipated commons renounced the title of our lord long ago. We served the crown, but had no noble in place as our local ruler."

"I know—that happened four hundred years ago! What's your point?"

"Just this, Your Majesty: my neighbors and I have discussed the matter, and we have judged that conditions have changed. That is to say, we'd like to change our minds."

"Change your minds? About what?"

"About renouncing our right to noble leadership. We've been thinking—it might be kind of nice to have a duke, or a baron or something. We don't really care what title you give him, but I think we want to give this local lord business a try."

Holt's mind reeled. Oxvale's status as an emancipated commons had been an important aspect of his life—and of all the other Darymen. Could they really bring themselves to give it up?

"I see." Dathwell's scowl darkened, but a glint of promise showed in his eye. "*I* choose the title—"

"But *we* choose the lord," Derek completed, bowing within the limits of his chair.

"We want Holt! Bearer of the Lodestone Blade,

and new Lord of Oxvale!" Nowell the Aching shouted, rising to his feet with startling agility and raising a glass to the cheers of his neighbors—and of all the others in the great hall.

Dathwell looked at the farmers, then at his daughter and the young knight. Holt stood still, not daring to draw a breath.

"The idea has promise . . ." began the king.

"Yes!" cried Danis. "We'll get married—you're a lord now, and Vanderthan couldn't hope to have a better king! We'll do it as soon as—"

Abruptly she halted, drawing slightly back from Holt and looking at him with her shining eyes. "That is . . . you know, I never really asked you if you *wanted* to marry me—I just told you what *I* would do." She blinked in consternation, and the Daryman smiled at her unusual reserve—the First Daughter of Vanderthan was not used to asking anyone for anything.

"Well?" she demanded in exasperation, after a brief pause. "*Do* you?"

His answer came in the form of another kiss, and not even the thunderous cheers of the gathered folk could drown out the sound of Holt's joy, ringing in his ears like a thousand bells.

Epilogue

"Well, that seemed to work out all right," Dalliphree said, sighing as she sat back on the bench. The waters of the goldfish pool swirled before her as she blinked back a tear.

"I should say—though it was a bit of a close thing, there with the dragon," Pusanth muttered. "I still say that artifact was a bad idea!"

"Well, at least it made things interesting," pouted the fairy. "And we didn't get into *that* much trouble!"

"Plenty enough for *me*!"

"And if it hadn't been for Karnach turning traitor

and telling everything to that red dragon, it would have been much easier. Imagine him trying to trick me into telling him about the crown—and then getting the princess to bring it right to him!"

"They *had* to go there anyway—remember?" Pusanth asked archly. "You're the one who made an artifact that could only be destroyed by dragon breath!"

"Well, it didn't have to be such a big, mean one!"

The sage's reply was bit back as another fellow came walking into the garden. The newcomer had a white beard, though not so long as Pusanth's, and his bright eyes looked about with a twinkle of humor and curiosity.

"Hello!" said Dalli. "Welcome to the garden of the immortals! You're new here, aren't you?"

"New? I should say so," said the fellow, plopping with the casual grace of a much younger man to another bench. "One moment I was standing in a cave, then—tut, tut—just a slight miscalculation. Now here I am!"

"Welcome," said Pusanth, formally. "I'm sure you'll find the surroundings quite peaceful—*most* of the time," he concluded, glowering at Dalliphree.

"Peaceful? Well, that would be a change," declared the new arrival. He looked curiously into the fish pool, then winked at Dalliphree.

"So tell me," he asked, a mischievous twinkle in his eye. "What do you do for fun around here?"